“I need someone—
Sweet Briar.”

Paul fought against a su
Cancer. Roz had cancer. It didn’t make sense. How could she be so sick?

Her face was as beautiful as ever, but the spark in her eyes had been replaced by fear and her brown skin looked dull. Her lips trembled as she tried to smile. Apparently her mouth refused to cooperate and after a moment she gave up the attempt.

“I know it will be inconvenient for you, but you’re my only hope. I’m determined to get well fast, so you shouldn’t have to stay for long. And Nathaniel is old enough to help with Megan and Suzanne.”

“I love my nieces and nephew. Of course I’ll come.”

Her body sagged in relief. “Thank you.”

“I’m trying to take everything one day at a time. Andrea and Edward are good and loving grandparents, and I know they’d step in if…”

“Don’t even think that way. You’re going to be fine. You’ll beat this. Focus all of your energy on getting well. I’ll take care of everything else.” She had to get better. Though he’d made a point of avoiding her the past dozen years, keeping out of her life, he couldn’t imagine a world without her in it.

* * *

SWEET BRIAR SWEETHEARTS:
There’s something about Sweet Briar…

Dear Reader,

Welcome back to Sweet Briar, North Carolina. If you read *Winning Charlotte Back*, you've already been introduced to Roz Martin and Paul Stephens, the heroine and hero of *The Single Mom's Second Chance*.

Roz and Paul have become two of my favorite people in Sweet Briar. Roz hasn't had an easy life and sadly her life is about to become even more difficult. She's a widowed single mother raising three kids, and her world is rocked when she receives a cancer diagnosis. Having no one else to turn to for help, she seeks out Paul, her former brother-in-law.

Paul has never forgiven Roz, his former high school sweetheart, for marrying his half brother. He's spent the past dozen years avoiding her as much as possible. The last thing he wants to do is see her every day. But he loves his nieces and nephew and they need him. Besides, he won't be able to look himself in the mirror if he turns his back on Roz. Having no choice, he moves in with her and her children.

I hope you enjoy reading Roz and Paul's story as much as I enjoyed writing it.

The Single Mom's Second Chance is the seventh book in my Sweet Briar Sweethearts series and my eighth overall. If you've missed any, visit my website, kathydouglassbooks.com, where there is a complete book list. While you're there, sign up for my monthly newsletter. I love hearing from my readers, so feel free to drop me a note.

Happy reading.

Kathy

The Single Mom's Second Chance

KATHY DOUGLASS

ISBN-13: 978-1-335-89475-5

The Single Mom's Second Chance

This edition published by arrangement with Harlequin Books S.A.

For questions and comments about the quality of this book, please contact us at CustomerService@Harlequin.com.

Harlequin Enterprises ULC
22 Adelaide St. West, 40th Floor
Toronto, Ontario M5H 4E3, Canada
www.Harlequin.com

Printed in U.S.A.

Kathy Douglass came by her love of reading naturally—both of her parents were readers. She would finish one book and pick up another. Then she attended law school and traded romances for legal opinions.

After the birth of her two children, her love of reading turned into a love of writing. Kathy now spends her days writing the small-town contemporary novels she enjoys reading.

Books by Kathy Douglass

Harlequin Special Edition

Sweet Briar Sweethearts

How to Steal the Lawman's Heart
The Waitress's Secret
The Rancher and the City Girl
Winning Charlotte Back
The Rancher's Return
A Baby Between Friends
The Single Mom's Second Chance

Furever Yours

The City Girl's Homecoming

To my husband and sons. You fill my life
with happiness. I love you with my entire heart.

To the reader. Whether this is the first of my books
that you're reading, the eighth or somewhere
in between, thank you for your support.
I appreciate you.

Prologue

Roz Martin stood in the hot June sun, staring at the building as if frozen in place. After three days of planning what she would say and determining the best way to approach Paul Stephens, her onetime high school sweetheart and brother-in-law, the energy that had propelled her this far ran out and she no longer had the strength to go inside. She tried envisioning the conversation, trying to picture a positive outcome, but she couldn't quite pull it off. Nothing in the recent past gave her reason to believe everything would work out. Sadly, nothing in the distant past gave her hope either.

Roz's eyes burned with angry tears. She'd sworn

she'd never be in this position again, yet here she was, once more dependent upon a person who didn't want anything to do with her. When she'd been five years old, she hadn't had a choice. Her parents had been killed in a car accident and her only living relative, her great-aunt, had become her legal guardian. But Aunt Rosemary had never wanted children and had only taken her in out of duty. She had provided Roz with a place to live and little else. Certainly not love or affection.

Now Roz had to come to Paul and beg for help. She hated it, but, once again, she didn't have a choice. She needed him. If she had to plead, then plead she would. Ever since the doctor had given her the bad news, she'd had to think of what was best for her children. This was simply one more instance of that. If it stung a little more, that was a price she was willing to pay.

Cancer. She had cancer. Just thinking the word filled her with dread and made her heart pound so hard her chest ached. She wanted to yell to the heavens about the unfairness of it all.

She'd never smoked. Didn't drink alcohol. She exercised regularly and maintained a diet filled with fresh fruits and vegetables. Yet, at thirty years old, she'd been diagnosed with stage II cervical cancer. Roz took a deep breath and steadied herself. Now wasn't the time for a pity party. Truthfully, there was never time in her life for self-pity.

She was a single mother of three wonderful children. Her three hearts. She'd do anything for them. Which was why, despite knowing how Paul felt about her, she'd packed up the kids and traveled from her home in Sweet Briar, North Carolina, to Tampa, Florida, to see him. A conversation like this was better had face-to-face.

She hadn't told the kids about her diagnosis yet. She knew the news would hit them hard and she didn't have the emotional strength to deal with that now. They believed that they were in town to wish their grandparents bon voyage before the couple set off on their delayed eight-month cruise in two days. In actuality, Roz had come to town to speak to Andrea, her mother-in-law, to get her help and advice.

Roz had told Andrea about her diagnosis and then sworn her to secrecy. Andrea had offered to postpone the cruise again, but Roz had turned her down. Although more than a year had passed since Roz's husband Terrence's sudden death, her father-in-law was still struggling with grief. Most days, Edward seemed to drift from place to place with nothing tethering him to his surroundings. Lately, he'd begun showing interest in the cruise they'd canceled after Terrence died and had been talking about their trip around the world. This vacation could be a turning point for him. There was no way Roz could ask them to put it off again and risk sending him spiraling back into sorrow. Especially when he would only worry about her. He'd been too good to her and her kids for her to even consider it. Which meant she had to ask Paul for help. That is, if she found the courage to step inside the health club he owned. Although her mother-in-law had offered to speak to Paul on her behalf, Roz had told her no. She wanted to stand on her own two feet.

The door swung open and two women dressed in brightly colored workout gear emerged. They spotted her and held the door open. Taking that as a sign to stop stalling, Roz smiled her thanks and trotted the last few feet down the concrete sidewalk.

"Have a good workout," one of the women said before walking away.

Not bothering to explain that she wasn't there to exercise, Roz murmured her thanks then stepped inside. Despite the weight of worry on her shoulders, she took a minute to look around. The reception area was spacious and buzzed with positive energy.

To her right, a large window revealed a Zumba class of about twenty women dancing to a Latin beat. To her left, doors led to dressing rooms and showers. A muscular man stood behind a curved desk in the middle of the reception area, greeting people as they scanned their membership cards before heading to locker rooms. About half a dozen people were sipping fresh juice smoothies at a bar. Roz hadn't expected to see this many people at midday on a Wednesday.

During their two-year relationship, Paul had spoken of his plans for the future. He'd always had an interest in physical training and planned of one day owning a gym. He'd more than accomplished that goal and now owned nearly twenty first-rate health clubs in three states. This was the first one he'd opened, and according to Andrea, he had an office here in addition to the one at his corporate headquarters. Today was the first time she'd been inside one of his clubs. Although she and Paul had been in-laws, they'd never been family.

Once, Roz had loved him with the entirety of her being. When they'd been dating, he'd made a lot of promises about their future which he'd promptly forgotten when he'd gone away to college. He'd forgotten her just as quickly, his calls to her growing fewer and farther between before they'd stopped altogether. College life and college girls had replaced her.

When she was eighteen, her aunt died, leaving her alone in the world. Paul had come home for the funeral and returned to school the following day. His older half brother, Terrence, started coming around, supporting Roz in the way she'd hoped Paul would. Terrence had given her a shoulder to lean on and been someone who'd listened to her worries. When he'd proposed, she'd said yes, relieved and grateful that she would no longer be alone. She'd cared a great deal for Terrence, but she hadn't been in love with him. They'd gotten married at city hall two weeks after he'd proposed.

Paul had never forgiven her.

Stepping up to the desk, Roz cleared her throat, drawing the attention of the receptionist. "Welcome to Build-A-Body. How may I help you today?"

"I'm here to meet with Paul Stephens."

"And your name?"

"Rosalyn Martin." Roz hadn't taken Terrence's name. Her maiden name was the only link she'd had to the parents she barely remembered.

The young man picked up a phone, and after a brief conversation where he'd alternated between looking at her and glancing through the window behind her, he smiled, then pointed toward the back of the building. "Mr. Stephens's office is up the stairs just behind the walking track. You can't miss it."

"Thank you." Roz strode around the desk and through the large gym area, stepping around the gleaming equipment. When she reached the stairs, she took a deep breath then blew it out slowly. The next few minutes would determine the course of the next months of her life. The pounding beat of the music blasting from unseen speakers couldn't drown out the sound of her heart slamming against her chest as she climbed the long flight of carpeted stairs. She'd thought there would be another reception area, but there wasn't. Instead, there was simply a long hallway that ended at a set of double doors.

Paul's name was etched on the nameplate attached to the wall beside them.

She knocked and waited until Paul called for her to enter before opening the door. He was sitting behind a massive desk that had been placed in front of a wall of windows overlooking the gym. He'd spun his chair around so that his back was to her. Although he must have heard her step inside, he made no move to face her. She stood still, refusing to utter a word until he acknowledged her presence. As he began to turn his chair around, she steeled herself for the conversation she needed to have.

"Roz." Paul's voice was so cold she all but shivered. She'd expected the displeasure; after all, he'd made his feelings plain over the past twelve years. There was no lingering affection between them. Still, her heart sank a little at the frown marring his handsome face. He wasn't going to make things easy for her.

She owned her part in their disastrous past, but he'd yet to do the same. To his way of thinking, she'd been 100 percent to blame for the demise of their relationship and he'd been the wronged party. It had never occurred to him that he'd let her down, too. Not that it mattered now. The only thing she cared about was ensuring her kids were cared for. If there was anyone else she could turn to, she would. She had friends in Sweet Briar of course, her best friend Charlotte Shields for one, but she didn't feel comfortable asking her to take on such a huge responsibility. She had a wedding to plan with the town doctor, Rick Tyler. Besides, like it or not, Paul was her children's uncle. He was their family and they were his. Family was supposed to take care of each other.

"Thank you for seeing me."

He grunted. "You didn't give me much choice, showing up here unannounced."

Maybe. But she knew he could have easily refused to see her and that would have been the end of it. Now that they were face-to-face, she wasn't sure how to start the conversation. She looked around his office. Though it was sparsely decorated, the tan leather furniture was appealing. A picture of Paul and a beautiful woman was on the corner of his desk. Although Roz and Paul weren't in each other's lives, from time to time, Andrea mentioned the women Paul dated and her hope that he'd finally settle down. Andrea seemed to believe that Kristin, Paul's girlfriend of seven months, was the one.

Maybe this wasn't the best idea after all. Seeing Paul as one half of a happy couple made her doubt her plan. He might not be willing to leave Kristin behind in Florida and come to North Carolina to help while Roz underwent chemotherapy and surgery. Her treatment and recovery would take months. Too bad she couldn't think of another solution.

Paul drummed his fingers on his desktop. "Do

you want to get to the reason you barged into my office today? I'm sure it wasn't just to look at me."

Roz's face grew hot as she struggled to keep from staring at him. As a teenager, he'd been dedicated to clean living and his body had reflected that. The years had been very good to him. He was six feet two inches of lean muscle. His brown skin glowed with good health, and his face was beyond handsome, even with his eyes narrowed with irritation.

She took a breath but the word cancer clogged her throat, leaving her unable to speak. To her horror, her eyes filled with tears and her vision blurred. Blinking back the moisture, she forced herself to talk. "I need your help."

"With what? Not that it matters. The answer is no. We don't have that type of relationship. Remember? If you'd thought it through, you could have saved yourself the trouble and me the time and aggravation."

"Are you still holding what happened when we were kids against me?"

"No. But I'm not willing to pretend that we're friends either. And since Terrence has died, we are no longer family." He made air quotes with his hands making it clear he'd never accepted her as part of the family.

"Do you consider my kids your nephew and nieces? Are they still your family? Do you still love them?"

"Of course I love them. What do they have to do with this favor of yours?"

"Everything. If not for them I wouldn't be interrupting your workday." The annoyed look on his face indicated that her time was coming to an end. Since there was no easy way to say it and she doubted the word would affect him the way it affected her, she just blurted it out. "I have cervical cancer."

He blinked and jerked as if she'd given him an electric shock. "What?"

"You heard me." She couldn't say it again. Her voice wobbled and one of the tears she'd tried so hard to hold back escaped and then slid down her face. She brushed it away, hoping he hadn't seen it. She didn't want Paul to see her cry. He might accuse her of using her tears as a weapon, and she wasn't prepared for that battle.

His mouth moved but no sound emerged. She could relate. She'd been floored when her doctor had delivered the news. Though she'd been sitting down, her knees had shaken like Jell-O in an earthquake. Even now, it was a struggle to stand. But she couldn't worry about his state of mind. She needed to get to the point of this meeting. "I'm going to be undergoing chemotherapy and having surgery soon."

When he simply stared at her, his face devoid of all expression, she continued. "I won't be able to take care of my kids. I have friends who will help me but that won't be enough. I'm going to need live-in help. Hiring someone is out of the question. I don't want my kids to have to adjust to a stranger in the house in addition to dealing with my illness. If there were someone else I could go to for help, I would. But there isn't. Your mother offered to postpone their cruise again, but I can't ask them to do that. Your father needs to get away from here in order to move past his grief and start living again. So I need someone—you—to come to Sweet Briar."

Paul's head was swimming and he fought against a sudden wave of dizziness. Cancer. Roz had cancer. The word echoed in his brain, then slammed repeatedly against his skull. It didn't make sense. How could she be so sick?

She looked fine. She'd always been slender, with small breasts, a tiny waist and slim hips, but, upon closer examination, she did appear a little thinner than she'd been at Terrence's funeral last year. Her white top was a bit loose and she kept adjusting the strap, preventing it from slipping off her shoulder. Although her face was as beautiful as ever, the spark in her eyes had been replaced by fear and her brown skin looked dull. Her lips trembled as she tried to smile. Apparently, her mouth refused to cooperate, and after a moment, she gave up the attempt.

"I know it will be inconvenient for you, but you're my only hope. I'm determined to get well fast, so you shouldn't have to stay for long. And Nathaniel is old enough to help with Megan and Suzanne."

It took a minute for her rapidly spoken words to register. Was she still trying to convince him? Was she that uncertain that she could rely on him? "Of course I'll come. Whatever you need."

Her body sagged in relief. "Thank you."

"Did you think I'd say no?"

"To be honest, I wasn't sure. I'd hoped you'd say yes but I came prepared to be turned down."

Considering that he'd initially said no before knowing what she needed, there was nothing he could say in his defense. "When did you get your diagnosis?"

"A week ago."

A week? And she hadn't said anything to him? "Why didn't you tell me sooner?"

Her eyes widened. "Are you kidding me? We haven't spoken a civil word to each other in years unless there was someone else around. As you just pointed out, we're neither family nor friends."

The words sounded so much crueler now. He'd been unnecessarily harsh. Shame battered him, leaving him speechless.

"My oncologist is working on a treatment plan. He'll have it together by Friday, with dates and schedules. I'll check with you before I confirm anything with him, to make sure you're available first."

"You don't have to do that. I'll be there whenever you need me to be."

"Just like that?"

"Just like that." It was true that they weren't friends. Too much had happened for them ever to be friends again. But he wasn't heartless. She and her kids needed him to step up and he would.

"Thank you. I appreciate it. If there was another way, I wouldn't inconvenience you like this."

"I love my nieces and nephew. I have a few things to clear up here and arrangements to make in order to work from North Carolina, so it may take me a couple of days. Will that work for you?" He was already mentally rescheduling meetings and rearranging plans for the next month or so. He'd adjust his schedule further out if necessary. And Kristin. He'd have to tell Kristin. Their schedules were so chaotic—she was a busy neurosurgeon and he was working tirelessly to build his business—that they rarely spent time together as it was. He'd prefer to have her blessing, but he was prepared to go to North Carolina without it.

"Whenever you arrive will be good. I need some time with the kids to prepare them for the future anyway."

"Did you tell them yet?"

"Not yet. We're spending the night with your parents and flying home tomorrow afternoon. I'll tell them tomorrow night or the next day."

"If you want, I can be there with you to reassure them that everything will be fine."

"That would be really great," she whispered. Tears filled her eyes and he felt her sorrow. Seeing her standing there, her arms wrapped around her middle, it struck him just how alone she was. How alone she'd been since Terrence's death.

Unable to contain himself, he went to her, taking her trembling hand into his. He tried his best to infuse her with his strength. "We'll get you through this. I promise."

"I'm trying to take everything one day at a time. Andrea and Edward are good and loving grandparents and I know they'd step in if..."

"Don't even think that way. You're going to be fine. You'll beat this. Focus all of your energy on getting well. I'll take care of everything else." She had to get better. Though he'd made a point of avoiding her the past dozen years, keeping out of her life, he couldn't imagine a world without her in it.

The unexpected thought stunned him. He might not want Roz to be sick, but there was no place for her in his world. There hadn't been for years.

Chapter One

The doorbell rang and Roz's heart skipped a beat. She'd watched from the window while Paul parked and then grabbed his luggage and briefcase from the rear of his SUV, yet she hadn't moved until the chimes filled her small house. She inhaled deeply, then went to the door. The time for hiding had passed. Now it was time to not only face Paul but to tell her kids about her cancer, as well.

Roz opened the door and then moved aside to let Paul step inside.

"How are you feeling?" he asked, setting his bags on the floor. He made a move in her direction and she froze. For a minute she thought he might hug her, but he didn't. After all these years of tension between them, an affectionate greeting would be weird. Even holding a civil conversation when they were alone felt strange.

"I feel fine. Absolutely fine." That was part of the reason she struggled to believe it when her gynecologist had given her the results of her Pap smear and subsequent biopsy. She hadn't experienced any symptoms. Not only that, she'd just turned thirty. Most women diagnosed with cervical cancer were much older than she was.

Not that the statistics changed anything. Her diagnosis had been confirmed so there was no use trying to make sense of it. She needed to accept the way things were and begin treatment. Fortunately, the cancer had been caught relatively early, which gave her a fighting chance of a full recovery.

"Good. Where are the kids?"

"Megan and Suzanne are helping me get dinner ready and Nathaniel is playing basketball with a friend."

"Do you need to pick him up?"

"No. His friend's dad is going to bring him home. He should be here in a few minutes."

"Did you tell the kids I was coming?"

"No." She'd started to, but then she couldn't think of a good reason why he would visit them when he hadn't before. Since she didn't want to lie to them, she decided to wait and tell them everything at once.

"Okay."

"Do you think I should have?"

"It's fine, Roz. Don't start worrying about something like that. They'll know in a little while."

She nodded. Paul was right. She needed to get a grip and stop stressing over little things or she'd scare the kids.

She led him farther into the house. He stepped closer and the heat from his body touched her, causing some of the icy fear in her heart to melt. Given the state of their relationship, that reaction made no sense. Still, she'd take a reduction in fear any day.

"Hi, Uncle Paul," Megan said, racing from the adjoining dining room, her arms open wide.

"Hi, Megan." He scooped her up into a big hug and grinned as she placed a kiss on his cheek. Although her and Terrence's relationship with Paul had been strained, they'd never prevented him from spending time with his nieces and nephew. As someone who'd grown up with only a great-aunt who'd resented having a kid foisted upon her, Roz wanted her children to have a bigger family and more love than she'd had. Since Paul loved them, she'd been willing to tolerate his distance. Besides, a small part of her had always hoped that, given time, they'd become friends again.

"What are you doing here?" Suzanne asked, following her sister into the living room.

"I came to visit you."

"But why do you have your suitcase? Are you going to sleep here?" Suzanne asked. At six years old, she didn't miss a trick. She was attuned to every little thing that happened in the house.

"Yes." He set Megan on her feet and then picked up Suzanne and gave her a hug. "Is that okay with you?"

She shrugged.

"It's okay with me, Uncle Paul," Megan said agreeably.

"Thanks, baby."

"I'm not a baby. I'm eight. That's a big girl."

"Okay. Thanks, big girl."

"And you two big girls need to set the table," Roz said. "We'll need five of everything."

The girls ran into the kitchen, leaving Roz and Paul alone. Though she'd felt comforted by his presence only a minute ago, she now felt awkward. Neither of them seemed to know what to say, so they stood there in uneasy silence. She gave herself a mental shake. This was her home and he was her guest. "Your room is all set. Come on."

He grabbed his bags and followed her up the stairs to the guest room.

After Terrence's death, Roz and the kids had needed a fresh start. The accounting office where she'd worked had had a vacancy for a CPA in their satellite office in the small coastal town of Sweet Briar, so Roz had sold their house in Raleigh and they'd relocated. She'd fallen in love with this charming four-bedroom house immediately. The kids hadn't cared about the house, but they'd been sold on the huge backyard and side yards. They'd made friends quickly and everyone had settled in nicely. Things had been going well until she'd found out she had cancer.

"This is a nice house. Different from the one you and Terrence had."

That house had been huge and modern. "It has all the space we need."

"I'm not kicking someone out of their room, am I?"

"No. The girls like sharing. They say it's like having a sleepover every night."

He laughed. "I'm glad they're so close."

He didn't say it, but Roz knew he was thinking about his own relationship with Terrence. The brothers hadn't been close at all. Terrence's mother had died when he was two and his father had fallen in love with Andrea shortly after that. They'd gotten married when Terrence was four. Paul had been born a year later. Andrea had loved Terrence as if she'd given birth to him and had never referred to him as her stepson. To her, he was her son. Terrence had loved Andrea in return. For a reason known only to himself, Terrence had always resented Paul. Those negative feelings had increased once Terrence and Roz had married. Only now, Paul returned the feelings. Roz had no proof, but she believed her past relationship with Paul had always bothered Terrence. None of it mattered now. Terrence was dead and Paul hated her.

"I'll get out of your way. Dinner will be on the table in about fifteen minutes."

"Okay. I'll meet you in the kitchen."

She left the room and was descending the stairs when the front door flew open and Nathaniel, her eleven-year-old son, stepped inside. He smiled broadly when he saw her. "Hi, Mom. Is dinner ready? I'm starving."

She gave him a quick hug. "Yep. We were just waiting for you."

Paul entered the room then. When Nathaniel saw him, his face lit up. "Hi, Uncle Paul. What are you doing here?"

"I came to visit my favorite nieces and nephew."

Nathaniel grinned. "We're your only nieces and nephew."

"True. But you're still my favorites."

"So I guess that makes Mom your favorite sister-in-law."

Nathaniel might not have noticed the second that passed before Paul replied, but Roz did. Although it was ridiculous, his hesitation pricked her heart. "Of course."

"Wash your hands, son."

"Okay, Mom."

Roz watched as Nathaniel ran into the first-floor powder room, leaving her alone with Paul. She didn't want to talk about anything personal, such as her being his supposed favorite sister-in-law. She didn't want to talk at all, but some things couldn't be put off. "I guess we should tell them after dinner."

"That sounds good to me." He looked at her, his eyes filled with compassion. "We'll get through this, Roz. One day at a time."

There was nothing to say to that, so Roz only nodded.

Dinner was not nearly as uncomfortable as Roz had expected it to be. The children were eager to catch Paul up on their lives and share their plans for the summer. After they'd eaten their dessert and put their dishes into the dishwasher, Roz hustled everyone into the living room.

Nathaniel sprawled on the floor in front of the television and the girls sat on the floor beside the coffee table, their closed coloring books in front of them. Paul sat beside Roz on the sofa, as if trying to infuse her with his strength. She appreciated the effort, but given the strain in their relationship, it was impossible. Though she was grateful for his willingness to put his life on hold to help her, they'd spent too many years at odds for there to be a psychic connection between them. Their relationship was rocky, to say the least, and their connection spotty at best. The years of being polite when necessary and ignoring each other when possible had taken their toll on their former closeness. Yet there was a part of her that yearned to lean on him. A part of her did find solace in his presence and drew strength from his nearness. Her mixed emotions reflected her relationship with Paul—it was a tangled mess.

"I want to talk to you all," Roz said.

"About what?" Suzanne asked.

"Is it somebody's birthday?" Megan asked hopefully. "I love cake and ice cream."

"I promise to clean my room tomorrow," Nathaniel joked.

"It's about me," Roz said. "I'm a little bit sick and I'm going to be having surgery. Uncle Paul is going to be staying with us until I'm better."

"What's wrong?" Nathaniel asked.

Roz had hoped to avoid saying the word cancer, but she knew now that it was impossible. Nathaniel was astute enough to notice if she avoided answering the question and would more than likely imagine the worst. If she just came out and said the word, acted like it was no big deal, maybe the kids wouldn't be as scared as if she tried to finesse it. So, rather than beat around the bush, she came out with it. "I have cancer. I know that's a scary word, but the doctors are going to work very hard to make me better. And I'm going to do everything they tell me to do. Some of the medicine might give me a stomachache, so don't be scared if you see me getting sick."

"Are you going to die?" Nathaniel's voice trembled, and Megan and Suzanne scooted close to each other and clasped hands. Her children's fear was heartbreaking in a way that nothing else could ever be. Having lost her own parents as a child, Roz understood the panic that lurked beneath her son's words. He'd already lost his father, a fireman, in a horrible fire that had taken three other lives. Losing her would cause more pain than any of her children should have to endure.

"I'm going to do my best to get well. People used to die from cancer, but the doctors have better medicine now."

"Medicine that is going to make you well." Megan's words were a declaration, but Roz knew her daughter was looking for confirmation that her world wouldn't be blown to smithereens. They all were.

"Yes." Roz hoped she was being honest. After all, the doctors had told her that they'd caught her cancer relatively early. It was localized and hadn't moved to her lymph nodes. They were optimistic, and she was doing her best to be so, too. Even if she was scared out of her mind, she wouldn't show her fear to her kids. They needed her to be strong. More than that, they needed to believe she was going to be fine. Most of all, they needed her. "The medicine is going to help me get well."

"But it's going to take time," Paul interjected. "And sometimes it might look like your mom is getting worse, but she won't be. She'll be getting better on the inside even if it doesn't look like that on the outside."

"And you're going to help Mommy?" Suzanne asked.

Paul covered Roz's hand and gave it a gentle squeeze. "Yes. Every day."

His words were a vow that Roz knew she could count on.

"And you aren't going to leave us?" Suzanne's voice quivered and Roz's heart crumpled as she fought back tears. This disease wasn't satisfied with attacking her body. Now it was trying to ravage her kids' hearts.

"No," Paul said firmly. He looked at each child. "I'm not going to leave you."

"Okay," Suzanne whispered.

Roz had been prepared for more questions, but her kids were silent. Rather than prod them to talk, she let them sit with the information, giving them time to process what they'd just learned in their own ways. Nathaniel turned on the television and the girls grabbed crayons and began flipping through their coloring books. Roz knew they hadn't been completely assured by the answers she and Paul had given them. They were overwhelmed and using the familiar to cope in a suddenly uncertain world.

Needing to do something, Roz went into the kitchen. The dishwasher was on the rinse cycle and the counters and tables had been wiped. The floor was clean, but she grabbed the broom anyway and began sweeping.

"I think they took it pretty well," Paul said as he came into the room.

Roz looked at him. She wasn't sure if he actually believed what he was saying or if he was humoring her. "I guess."

He shoved his hands into the pockets of his cargo shorts and leaned against the wall. Clearly, he wasn't going anywhere. Despite all the history between them and her anxiety, she couldn't help but notice the way his shirt pulled tight against his muscular chest. She frowned. Her days of being attracted to Paul ended when he left her behind all those years ago.

"What do you want?" she asked. He reeled back as if she'd struck him, and she blew out a breath. It wasn't his fault that she'd felt the slightest—and unwanted—zing of attraction. "Sorry. I didn't mean to bite your head off."

"It couldn't have been easy telling them. I just wanted to make sure that you're okay."

"I'm fine." He looked at her for so long she became uncomfortable. She'd grown accustomed to Paul looking through her, so this new scrutiny was unnerving. Her skin began to tingle as he only continued to stare. "Why are you looking at me like that?"

"I don't know if you're fine or not. I can't read

you the way I used to. However, given the fact that you're sweeping a floor that has just been swept, I'm leaning toward no. This isn't going to work if you hide your feelings."

"You're here for my kids. I can handle my feelings on my own."

He shook his head. "I'm here for all of you. Your feelings and welfare matter to me, too."

That was different. He hadn't cared about her feelings in the past. In fact, he'd hurt them quite often. But now that she had cancer, he was suddenly Mr. Sensitive. He might be able to pretend the past away, but she wasn't interested in playing that game.

She doubted he really cared. He was simply saying what was expected in this situation. He could keep his insincere words. She'd prefer honesty, even if it was painful.

"I'm fine," she said firmly. She leaned the broom against the wall then returned to the front room. If her kids needed to act like tonight was a regular night, she would join them. Besides, it would help her keep her distance from Paul, something she desperately needed to do. She was vulnerable now and didn't want to confuse his obligation with a heartfelt emotion that would only lead to hurt and disappointment.

Paul put the last T-shirt in the dresser drawer, then closed his empty suitcase and shoved it into the closet. It was smaller than the walk-in one in his condo, but it would do. He hadn't given much thought to his clothes; his mind had been elsewhere. Since the weather was warm, he'd packed mostly shorts and a couple pairs of jeans. He'd brought a suit, too, although he doubted he'd wear it.

"Uncle Paul?"

He turned and smiled at Nathaniel. "Hey."

"I want to talk to you."

Nathaniel's expression was serious, so despite being tired, Paul didn't want to put him off until tomorrow. "How about we go outside? Your mom and sisters are probably already asleep and we don't want to disturb them."

Nathaniel nodded. He didn't say a word until they were sitting on the front porch steps. Even then, the crickets were the only sound for several minutes.

Paul decided to jump-start the conversation. "What's up?"

"I'm eleven."

"I know."

"I can take care of Mom and my sisters. You can go back to Florida. I don't need your help."

Paul hadn't expected that, but perhaps he should have. Paul had always been protective of his mother even though she'd had a husband by her side to take care of her. Nathaniel no longer had a father, and, in his mind, he was the man of the house. As her oldest child, Roz might rely on Nathaniel to help with his sisters, but Paul knew that she was doing her best to guard his childhood. There was no way she would burden him with adult concerns. That she'd sought out Paul proved that.

"Everyone needs help now and then."

"You just think I'm a kid and can't do it."

"No. I think you're a kid and shouldn't have to do it. Your mom knows how great you are. And I know how much you help her with the girls. We want you to keep doing that. But at the same time, I'm here so that you can have fun doing things you enjoy. Like playing basketball with your friends and riding your bike."

"I can do those things and still take care of Mom."

Paul knew he had to tread carefully so he didn't hurt Nathaniel's feelings and put him on the defensive. Things would go more smoothly if they worked together. He just had to get Nathaniel to see that they were on the same side. They both wanted to help Roz.

Though Nathaniel believed he was equipped to handle the job of caretaker, Paul knew better. The kid was too young to handle so much responsibility. "I'm sure you can. And I'm counting on you. It's going to take both of us working together to make sure that your mom gets all the care she needs and that the girls don't get left behind."

Nathaniel gave him a look that let Paul know he

hadn't convinced him. But words wouldn't get rid of Nathaniel's skepticism. Only actions would do that.

Nathaniel opened his mouth, but Paul was tired and didn't want to go around in circles for the rest of the night. He'd been working practically around the clock organizing his business so he could work from Sweet Briar and he'd barely slept in days. "How about we just give it a try?"

"I don't need to play basketball or ride my bike."

"Maybe you don't need to do those things, but we have to keep things normal for Megan and Suzanne. They need to know that it's okay to have fun. If you stop playing, they might get worried and think your mother is sicker than she is. That might scare them. You don't want to do that, do you?"

Nathaniel shook his head.

"Good. It's best for the girls for everything to be the same as it was before."

"Except you weren't here before."

"No. But if you act like it's okay for me to be here, then it won't seem unusual to them. You're the big brother. The girls are going to follow your lead. If you're all right, they'll be all right."

Nathaniel rubbed his hands over his shorts. "Will you tell me the truth about something?"

"Yes."

Nathaniel's voice quivered. "Is Mom going to die?"

Paul's throat tightened and he felt like he was

being strangled. It took maximum effort to make his voice sound normal. "I don't think so. She has good doctors and she's going to do everything they tell her to do so that she can get well."

"And you think she will," Nathaniel pressed.

"Yes." Paul hoped that he wasn't giving the kid false hope. But worrying him unnecessarily didn't make sense.

"Okay." Nathaniel stood. Instead of going into the house, he turned and glared at Paul. "You'd better be telling me the truth."

After Nathaniel marched into the house, Paul looked up at the darkening sky. He hoped what he said was the truth. Otherwise, they all would be in a world of hurt.

Chapter Two

Roz slid onto the step and then leaned her head against the rail, closing her eyes and praying that the dizziness would pass. She'd undergone her first chemotherapy session in Charlotte yesterday and she was weak. Paul was dropping the kids at the youth center where they would spend the day, so she didn't have to put on a good face for them. It had been a week since she'd told the kids about her illness, but they hadn't brought it up again. She didn't know if that was good or bad, but she didn't feel good enough to start a conversation about her health with them.

Her kids loved playing with their friends at the youth center and spent several days a week there.

With Paul's help, the kids could stick to their normal routine, which wouldn't leave them time to worry about her. Normal was what she was striving for.

She'd kissed each of her children goodbye and managed to stay upright on the sofa until they were out the door. Then, summoning all of her energy, she'd tried to return to her bedroom. She'd crossed the living room and climbed six of the thirteen stairs leading to the second floor before her energy had run out.

Frustrated, sad and scared, Roz let the tears that had been building up slide down her face. There was no one to see her and no reason she had to hide her feelings. No need to fake the serenity she was nowhere near feeling.

Roz heard the front door open and swiped a hand across her face. Paul was back more quickly than she'd expected. There was no way she wanted him to see her crying. He already felt sorry for her. She didn't want more of his pity. She didn't want his pity at all.

"Are you okay?" Paul asked as he jogged up the stairs, two at a time.

"I'm fine."

"Why are you sitting here?"

"I got tired. I'm better now." She pushed to her feet. It was slow going and she wobbled.

"You're not better," Paul said, sweeping her into his arms and carrying her the rest of the way up the stairs. He didn't put her down until he reached her room and set her on the side of her bed.

"Thank you," she said begrudgingly. She wasn't angry with Paul. Not really. But being carried only emphasized how dependent she was on him.

If Paul noticed her unpleasant tone, he chose to ignore it. "You didn't eat much breakfast. Do you want to try and eat a little bit more?"

"What I really want to do is go back to sleep. Then maybe I'll eat something."

He didn't look pleased by her answer, but he didn't try to change her mind. She appreciated that. Just because she was dependent on him for help didn't make her a child. "I'll let you sleep, then. I'll be back in a couple of hours. If you need anything, just call."

She nodded and pointed to her cell phone. He'd programmed his number into her phone that first night even though he could hear her if she yelled. She waited until he'd gone back downstairs before crawling into her bed and placing her head on her pillow. Hopefully, a nap would energize her before the kids got home.

Paul cleared the breakfast dishes with jerky movements. Though he worked efficiently, his thoughts were elsewhere. There was no way Roz was going to be able to climb those stairs every day. True, she'd had chemotherapy yesterday, and might get her strength back soon, but what if she didn't? In his research, he'd learned that, for some people, the side effects from chemo could last for days or weeks. What if Roz was one of those people? Her treatment plan called for her to undergo chemo every three weeks. She was scheduled for four treatments. She could be sick and weak for months. And that didn't include surgery and recovery times.

There had to be something he could do.

He returned the syrup to the walk-in pantry and paused before going through the kitchen into the tiny catchall room that shared a wall with the pantry. The idea hit him instantly. He could knock down the wall between the rooms and create a main floor bedroom for Roz. That way she wouldn't need to go up and down the stairs. He'd worked with a builder the summer before he'd left for college and had learned a lot. First, he needed to make sure that the wall wasn't structural. If it wasn't, the process would be a lot cheaper and go a lot faster. And it would make life easier for all of them.

Living with Roz and her kids was nothing like he'd thought it would be. To be honest, he hadn't given it any thought before agreeing to come and help her. Hearing the word cancer had struck fear in his heart like he'd never experienced before. Although he tried not to show it, he was still worried about her.

Once she'd left his office, he'd scoured the internet for every article he could find about cervical cancer. What he'd read confused him. Most cases of cervical cancer occurred in middle-aged women. Roz was only thirty.

He hadn't taken much time to think about the details of the move. There'd been too much to do. He might not understand her medical condition, but he knew one thing. She needed him.

The easiest tasks had been work related. Although he delegated work to his trusted vice president, Paul was a hands-on owner. He liked to know what was going on in his business. To him, being visible and accessible were key, so he visited each of his locations every quarter to talk with employees and mingle with members. All told, he spent roughly ten days a month on the road, so his absence wouldn't be a problem. His office staff assured him they could function on their own.

But talking with Kristin hadn't gone as smoothly. Though she was beautiful, it was her logical nature that he found most attractive. She was always levelheaded and rational. Kristin was a brilliant surgeon with a compassionate heart, but she wasn't the emotional type. That's why Paul had been so surprised by her response to his decision to help Roz. She'd blown her top. She claimed she understood Roz's need for assistance. She just hadn't understood why Paul was the one who had to help her.

They'd gone around in circles without coming to an understanding. Neither had been able to convince the other. He'd been ready to table the conversation and discuss it once their tempers had cooled, but Kristin had said it would be best if they stopped seeing each other. That had seemed extreme to him, but she'd been adamant. He'd reluctantly agreed, but he wasn't ready to let that relationship die. He believed that, given time, she'd realize that he was right.

But in the meantime, was it wise to get so involved with Roz's problem that he was renovating her house? Maybe not, but what choice did he have?

Nathaniel was old enough to help him. That would give them a chance to bond. The girls had chattered away on the drive to the youth center that morning. Apart from giving directions or answering one of his sister's questions, Nathaniel hadn't said a word. Apparently, the easy relationship they'd once shared was a thing of the past. Nathaniel was a good kid, so Paul didn't expect his attitude to last long. Working together to build the room and make Roz's life better would help them get back on good terms.

Paul spent the rest of the morning measuring the spaces and sourcing and pricing materials. He even sketched a design to share with Roz. Hopefully, she would agree to his plan.

When he was done, he warmed up soup and made sandwiches for them. Balancing everything on a tray, he headed to Roz's room. She was sitting up in her bed and color had returned to her face. Her eyes were alert. Seeing her looking so normal eased the tight band that had been squeezing his chest since he'd spotted her on the stairs earlier.

"I brought you lunch."

She eyed the tray. He was completely aware of the moment she noticed there were two bowls of soup and two sandwiches, but other than raise her eyebrow, she didn't react. There was no reason for the two of them to eat together—they only shared a meal when the kids were around—but he wanted to talk to her about his plan.

"I can't eat all of that."

"Try. Once you take a few bites, your appetite might return."

"That's not how it works."

He knew that. But he couldn't just let her waste away. She hadn't eaten anything after her chemotherapy yesterday and she'd barely eaten breakfast today. He'd badgered her into taking a few bites of banana and she'd gnawed on a piece of toast, just to get him to shut up.

"Food is fuel."

"You should know."

He waited until she sipped a spoonful of soup before broaching the subject of the room. "I've been thinking."

"Again? That's what, twice this year? You need to watch out for that. If you do it too often, it might become a habit. Then where would you be?"

He laughed and nearly choked on his sandwich.

He'd forgotten just how wicked her sense of humor was. Given everything going on with her health, it was good that she could still make jokes, even if it was at his expense. "I'll be as careful as I can."

She nodded and slurped some more soup.

"I was thinking about knocking down the wall between the pantry and storage room and making a bedroom for you downstairs. Then you won't have to deal with the stairs."

She stared at him, her previous mirth gone. "That sounds like a lot of effort and time. Not to mention money."

"It's not."

"Not what? A lot of money or a lot of effort and time."

"All of the above. If you're interested in the room, Nathaniel and I can build it."

"Nathaniel? He's just a kid. He already has more responsibility than he needs. He should be playing with his friends, not working construction."

"I agree. But that's not the way he sees it. He looks at my presence as a threat to his role in the family. Building the room together would help him see me less as a threat and more like a friend."

Roz sighed. "I suppose so. How much do you think it'll cost?"

"I'll pay for it, Roz. It was my idea after all."

"I have money. I'm on paid sick leave. Plus I have disability insurance. I don't need your charity."

"It's not charity. Consider it my rent."

"Rent?"

"I'm not paying anything, yet I'm using your electricity and water. Seems like a fair trade."

"You're taking care of my kids."

He was taking care of her, too, but obviously she couldn't bring herself to admit that. "They're my nieces and nephew."

"Still..."

The last thing either of them needed was a long, drawn-out argument. The new room was supposed to make her life easier, not more stressful. "Let me do this for you, Roz. It's a gift. But if you can't accept it as that, you can pay for the materials. How's that?"

She nodded. "I appreciate the thought. And a room downstairs would make sense. At least in the short term. It could serve as a guest room or office, down the road."

After that, they sat in awkward silence for a little while. Years of talking to each other only when required had killed their previous ability to communicate easily, and their earlier camaraderie had vanished. He searched for something to say. "How often do the kids go to the youth center?"

"It depends. On average, I'd say three or four times a week. They'd go every day if I let them."

"How late do they stay?"

"They had been staying most of the day. Remember, I have a job and can't leave them home alone all day."

He covered her hand with his and forced himself to ignore the spark of electricity that made his skin tingle. "Hey, I'm not criticizing you. I'm just trying to get a handle on their schedule so I can work around it."

She pulled away her hand and tucked it under the blanket. "You don't need to work around their schedule. I'll be able to take them most days. And I should be able to go back to work, too."

"We'll see."

"We'll see? Aren't you the one constantly telling me I'll be fine? Now it's 'we'll see'?"

"It's a process, Roz. It'll take time. That's all I'm saying. Don't be impatient."

"Impatient?"

"Yes. You never liked waiting for things. You're thirty years old. You should have learned patience by now." If she would have waited for him to graduate from college, they could have gotten married. He'd planned to come back for her. Of course, that presumed she'd actually loved him. She'd married Terrence fast enough. He shoved that irritating thought aside. Now wasn't the time to dig up the bones of their dead relationship. In fact, there was never a time for that. The past needed to stay six feet under.

She compressed her lips. "Apparently not. I've

run out of patience for this conversation. Now, if you don't mind..."

She didn't say the words, but he heard them anyway. Get out.

"On that note, I'll leave. Call me if you need anything."

A grunt was her only response, so he grabbed the tray and left. Now he remembered why they hadn't talked in all these years.

Roz leaned back on the sofa, listening to the hammering coming from the back of the house. She picked up one of the mysteries Charlotte had given her when she'd stopped by to visit earlier. They'd discussed Charlotte's wedding plans. Roz still couldn't believe that Charlotte was marrying the man who'd left her at the altar twelve years ago. But if Charlotte could forgive Rick, then maybe Paul would one day get past his anger at Roz.

It had been two weeks since Paul and Nathaniel had begun working on the room. Two weeks where she and Paul had walked on eggshells. They were being exceedingly polite to each other, avoiding topics that could lead to conflict. Paul didn't ask her about her emotions again. Since she'd told him she could handle her own feelings, she shouldn't be hurt. Yet she felt a little disappointed that he hadn't tried harder to discover how she felt. But she wasn't going to volunteer the information.

Truth was, she didn't know how she felt. Her feelings changed with the day. Or, more accurately, they changed several times a day. She tried to maintain a positive demeanor for her kids, but that was exhausting. Add in the effects of the chemotherapy, which, unfortunately, she was still feeling, and she was at the proverbial end. In that sense, it was better that she and Paul didn't talk often. If he caught her at the wrong time, there was no telling what she would say.

She'd been surprised when Paul offered to build the room for her. Now she wondered if that was a way of keeping his distance from her. After all, she couldn't help him tear down walls or rip up old floors. She barely had enough energy to cook a full meal. He could spend hours in there away from her and she couldn't object, because he was doing it to help her.

"They're making a lot of noise," Suzanne complained, covering her ears and leaning into Roz's side. "I don't like it."

"I'm sorry, baby. If it was nicer we could sit outside," Roz said. A hard rain had been falling since last night and didn't look like it would stop anytime soon. The gloom from outside had seeped into the house, making both girls cranky. It was too early for them to take a nap, so Roz was trying, without success, to keep them occupied. They'd already watched their favorite Disney movie and dressed and undressed their dolls. Neither girl had much interest in video games or playing on Roz's tablet although she'd offered it to them.

"I wish I could help like Nathaniel, but Uncle Paul won't let me," Megan said, her bottom lip poking out. Megan always tried to keep up with her brother. Nathaniel was good-natured and generally didn't mind her trailing behind him. But Paul had insisted that a construction zone was nowhere for the girls and wouldn't let them anywhere near the room. He'd told them they could help decorate, but that promise was too distant for Megan.

Much to Nathaniel's delight, Paul had allowed him to help tear down the wall. They'd hung new drywall, painted and refinished the floor. Now they were nailing the trim into place. If all went according to plan, she would be able to sleep in her new room tomorrow night.

"Uncle Paul will let you help once this part is done. In the meantime, how about we finish our puzzle?" Roz and the girls were working on a 350-piece puzzle that Paul had brought home last week.

"Okay, Mommy."

The girls ran into the dining room where the pieces were spread out on the table. Roz followed more slowly. She was nauseous, and even walking that short distance took more out of her than she wanted to admit. Although she'd expected to be weak, she still hated the feeling and tried to push through it. "Fake it until you make it" was becoming her new motto. Too bad it didn't work. It turned out her willpower wasn't stronger than the side effects of chemo.

Megan chattered happily as they worked, her disappointment at not being able to help Paul temporarily forgotten. Roz tried to pull Suzanne into the conversation, but with little success. Much to Roz's dismay, her previously happy and outgoing youngest child was drawing into herself more each day. At six years old, she was old enough to know that her mother was seriously ill, but too young to process the knowledge in a way that made sense to her. Roz hadn't yet discovered a way to help Suzanne express her feelings.

"Come see your new room," Nathaniel said, charging into the dining room and then out again. Roz had gotten so used to the hammering that she hadn't noticed when it stopped.

Megan shot to her feet and raced off behind her brother. Suzanne took her time getting up from her chair, but she eventually followed them. Roz had gotten a bit stiff, and she was slow to rise.

"Let me help you," Paul said, coming up behind her. Before she could protest, he'd slipped his arm around her waist and helped her stand. Once she was steady on her feet, she stepped out of his embrace, but not before his scent, a combination of perspiration and paint, filled her senses.

Roz was having a hard time adjusting to the new

Paul. Over the years she'd become used to the distant, cold Paul. The unforgiving Paul. This considerate man confused her, and she had to remind herself not to be deceived by his manners. Paul didn't like her. He'd made that abundantly clear over the years. He was no different from her aunt, who'd taken her in out of duty. He didn't care for her any more than Aunt Rosemary had. He was just better at hiding his feelings than her aunt had been. He was just doing what was expected of him.

Paul reached for her and she swatted his hand away. "I can make it on my own. It's only a few feet from here."

This house had always felt cozy. With Paul staying here, the rooms had gone from cozy to tiny. Despite the fact that they spent a good deal of their time in different rooms, there was never a waking moment when she wasn't acutely aware of his presence, which left her jumpy and uneasy. Lately, he'd begun to invade her dreams, taking away even that small haven.

"I'm sure you can. I'm just here as backup."

Roz decided no response was required and walked away. She'd made it halfway across the kitchen and was heading towards the closed door leading to her new bedroom when Nathaniel stepped out and shut the door behind him. "Close your eyes, Mom."

"How am I supposed to see where I'm going?"

"I'll help," Paul said, stepping closer. She'd tried

to pretend that he hadn't been a breath away, but with his arm securely wrapped around her waist, the heat from his body encircling her, that fantasy was swept entirely away and another one tried to replace it.

"Don't let me bump into the door," Roz warned as if it were a real possibility.

"I'll hold it open," Nathaniel promised. "But first, close your eyes."

Roz closed her eyes and allowed Paul to steer her around the kitchen table and chairs. Hadn't she just thought her rooms had shrunk since Paul had come to stay with them? Now her kitchen seemed as large as a football field. When they reached the door, she brushed past Nathaniel and stepped into her new room.

"You are going to be so happy, Mommy," Megan exclaimed.

"Can I open my eyes now?"

"Yes."

Roz looked around and gasped. She didn't know what she'd expected, but it certainly wasn't this magnificent room. Without the wall separating the two spaces, the room was quite big. Paul had refinished the old oak floors, and they glistened. The walls were painted a soft butter color and the trim matched the floor.

"Do you like it?" Nathaniel asked.

"I love it. Thank you so much." She pulled him into a tight hug and kissed his cheek.

"It wasn't just me," he said. "Uncle Paul helped."

Roz looked at Paul. There was no way she was hugging or kissing him. "Thank you."

"You're quite welcome." His voice was quiet, but she heard the sincerity there.

"But it's empty," Suzanne said, turning in a slow circle. "How are you supposed to sleep in here when you don't have a bed?"

Paul scooped Suzanne into his arms, and she wrapped her arms around his neck. "We're going to bring your mom's bed down here."

"And her dresser? And chair?"

"We're going to bring down everything."

"I want to help," Megan said.

"Of course you can help. You'll be in charge of bringing down the books."

"I'll start now," Megan said.

Paul halted her before she could dart from the room. "How about we start after we eat? Breakfast was a long time ago and my stomach is growling."

The girls giggled. Suzanne leaned back so she could look directly into Paul's eyes. "You're so silly, Uncle Paul."

"I'm hungry, too," Nathaniel added.

"I'll make lunch," Roz said, backing from the room. Seeing how well Paul fit with her family made her stomach flutter ridiculously. She needed to escape before that feeling grew.

"I'll take care of that," Paul said. "I'm here to help after all."

"I can make sandwiches for my own kids."

"I know you can. But how about the girls and I take care of lunch and Nathaniel can tell you everything he learned about construction."

"Yeah," Nathaniel said, taking Roz by the hand and leading her from the room. If she didn't know better, she'd think he and Paul had plotted the entire thing to keep her from overexerting herself.

"Fine," Roz agreed. Not that she had much choice. Paul was nothing if not determined. With the kids on his side, she didn't stand a chance. Since he was doing exactly as she'd asked, she had no right to complain.

If she was honest, the problem wasn't with him. It was with her. She liked being able to rely on him. She liked the way he was with the kids. She liked the kind way he treated her.

And that was a problem she needed to solve before she got used to having him around. Because, sooner or later, Paul was going to go back to Florida, leaving her behind again. This time she had no intention of being heartbroken.

Paul watched Nathaniel steer Roz into the front room then turned to the refrigerator.

"What are we making, Uncle Paul?" Megan asked.

"I thought we could have turkey sandwiches, tomato soup and salad."

"I don't want a salad," Suzanne said. "And I don't want soup and sandwich either. I want cake and ice cream. And potato chips."

"Those are snacks and desserts, not lunch. You need to eat real food so you can grow big and strong."

"I don't want that and you can't make me eat it."

Paul sighed. This was so unlike Suzanne, who was usually a sweet girl. Over the past couple of weeks, he'd noticed how much she'd changed. She cried when she didn't get her way and didn't talk as much as she used to. She'd begun sucking her thumb again, a habit Roz had told him she'd broken years ago. Since there had been a lot of changes in her life, her behavior wasn't entirely unexpected. She needed his patience and understanding. "No, I can't. But how about you eat chips with your salad and sandwich? And, after dinner, you can have ice cream for dessert. How does that sound?"

"That sounds good," Megan said then gave her younger sister a meaningful look. "Don't you think that sounds good, Suzanne?"

Suzanne didn't look quite convinced, but much to Paul's relief, she nodded.

The girls "helped" him prepare lunch, and then they all sat down together to eat. Roz didn't have much of an appetite these days and she ate even less than Suzanne did. Still, it was better than nothing.

Nathaniel was still hyped over the work he'd done, and his and Megan's conversation filled what otherwise would have been an uncomfortable silence. After eating, they carried their dishes to the sink and then scattered. As Paul loaded the dishwasher, he blew out a long sigh.

Another day nearly done and countless more left. He just hoped he would survive them.

Chapter Three

"Hurry up," Nathaniel said to his sisters. "Miss Joni will be here in a minute."

"We still have time," Roz said, waiting as Megan chose the ribbons and barrettes she wanted in her hair. Joni Danielson, the director of the youth center, had arranged for the kids to spend the day on a neighboring ranch and had personally offered to take them there. Nathaniel was so excited about the trip and the prospect of riding a horse that he'd been pacing the house for nearly an hour, unable to sit still. "Why don't you wait on the porch and let me know when she gets here?"

"Okay." Nathaniel was out the door before the words were out of her mouth.

"What if the horses are scary?" Suzanne asked.

"I don't think they'll be scary," Roz said, tying the chosen purple ribbon in a bow. "I think they'll be nice. You'll have fun riding them."

"Are you sure?"

"Yes. You guys are going to have the best time. I want to hear all about it."

"I'm going to tell you everything, Mommy," Megan promised.

"Thank you. I can't wait."

"Miss Joni's here," Nathaniel called, running back into the house, the door slamming behind him.

"Did you leave her standing on the porch?" Roz asked.

"No. She's getting out of her car."

"I'll let her in," Paul said.

A few minutes later, Joni and the kids were on their way to the Double J Ranch, leaving Roz alone with Paul. She'd expected him to use this quiet time he had to catch up on work. She knew he spent a few hours each night working once the kids were in bed. He had to be tired from burning the midnight oil. Instead, he sat beside her as if he had all the time in the world.

"How are you feeling today?"

"Fine," she answered automatically. Two weeks had passed since her second chemo treatment and she was already dreading the third. What good would it do to mention that, even on her best days, she never felt good anymore. Not just physically, but emotionally. She was beginning to forget what good actually felt like. Despite her best efforts to think positively, there was always that nagging knowledge that a full recovery wasn't guaranteed. The possibility remained that one day she might not be there for her children.

And she wouldn't even get to the vanity part. Seeing Joni looking so good, her long hair pulled back into a ponytail, Roz had felt like a scarecrow. Her own once-thick hair had begun to thin and, worse, was breaking off and coming out in patches. It seemed that every morning she awoke to discover clumps of hair on her pillow. At this rate, she would be bald in a week. Now Roz could barely stand to look in the mirror.

"You don't have to hang out with me," she said. "I know you have work to do."

"I have a few minutes."

She couldn't tell him to leave without being rude, but she didn't want to talk about herself, so she decided to turn the conversation to him. "We've never really talked about this, but I've been wondering. How did you get started in the health club business?"

He rubbed a hand over his head. "When I was in college, I was angry and frustrated a lot. I needed a constructive way to blow off steam, so I started going to this gym near campus and lifting weights. I didn't have good form, but I didn't care.

"This older guy, Stuart, was always there. One day he gave me some tips and helped me set up a complete program. After a while I found myself baring my soul to him. When I told him about the difficult relationship I had with my father, he didn't make excuses for Dad. Most of the time he just listened while I vented. Later, I learned that he owned the gym.

"After a while, he offered me a part-time position. I started out sweeping the floors and working the front desk. When I graduated, he sold me half of the gym. Two years later, I bought him out and expanded. It was a lot of work and some good fortune, but now I own nineteen locations. I'm opening three more this fall. My team is always scouting places where one of the gyms will prosper."

He'd always had a head for business, but she'd never imagined he'd be so successful so quickly. "Impressive."

"Thanks."

"I hope being here isn't harming your business."

"It isn't. I have a good team. They don't need me looking over their shoulders in order to do their jobs. And we communicate well, which keeps misunderstandings and errors to a minimum. But you know something about the danger of miscommunication, don't you?" He blew out a breath. "I just wish you would have told me."

Told him what? About Terrence? Why would he mention that now? No good would come from that discussion.

Perhaps that was why they stuck to surface topics where there was no danger of dredging up emotions. You couldn't get your feelings hurt if you never got close to them. Now they were sitting in awkward silence, with no knowledge of how to fill it.

Mercifully, his cell phone rang. "I'll let you get that," she said. "I'm going to sit outside for a while."

He nodded as he answered the phone and headed to the kitchen. When she reached the porch, she sat on the swing. Her mind replayed what he'd said and she began to read between the lines.

He'd felt betrayed. That had to be it. He'd been angry when she'd married Terrence. At the time, she'd thought she no longer mattered to him. After all, he'd stopped calling her and was never around when she called him. Now she wondered if he'd really cared about her back then. Even though it shouldn't matter now, and it didn't change the past, she still felt better believing that he hadn't just forgotten about her.

At the time, she'd felt so alone. So lost. Believing that she'd been easily forgotten had damaged her soul in ways that, even now, she couldn't voice. Knowing that it wasn't true was the balm her heart needed to help her heal from a hurt she'd tried to, but never could, overcome.

Why did he just tell her that? Although they'd been living in the same house for over a month, he'd seen to it that they'd never discussed anything personal. At least not pertaining to him. Yet for a reason unknown to him, he'd found himself sharing his past with her. Luckily for his pride, he hadn't told her how distraught and grief-stricken he'd been.

Before Paul had met Stuart, he'd never told anyone about his relationship with his brother and father. It had hurt his soul to be the insignificant second son of the second wife. In a way, Stuart had become the father Paul had always wanted. If not for him, Paul doubted he would have any type of relationship with his father. But he'd gotten over the bitterness and come to accept his father for who he was. Edward wasn't going to change, so Paul had needed to adjust his expectations.

Even now, his father mourned Terrence's death in a way that made it clear he'd lost his favorite child. Paul understood how devastated his father must have been when he'd learned of Terrence's death because he'd been hurt himself. But there were times over the past year when he'd watched Edward wall himself off from his family that Paul had wanted to yell at him and remind him that he still had a son.

Of course, that would have been futile. Edward

didn't want Paul's comfort. He'd wanted Terrence. So Paul had left Edward to grieve in his own way. It was only in the past few months that Edward had begun to live a little, and taking the delayed cruise was a big part of that. Paul's mother sent postcards and pictures from just about every port, so Paul knew his father was enjoying himself. Getting away had been good for his parents, even if their vacation had come at an inopportune time.

Andrea had made a couple of phone calls to check on Roz's health. Both Roz and Paul assured her that things were going well and encouraged her to enjoy the rest of the once-in-a-lifetime cruise. Paul could take care of everything.

Speaking of taking care of everything, the kids would be home soon and there was dinner to prepare. He shut off his computer and then went to the kitchen. Roz was in there, grabbing things from the refrigerator and placing them on the counter. He leaned against the wall and silently watched her. Though she moved slowly, she still possessed the grace that had always entranced him. She was humming a song he didn't recognize.

She glanced up and spotted him. "Hey."

He pushed off the wall and took a seat at the table. Though it would be polite to offer to help her, he knew she wouldn't take his offer in the spirit it was intended. If positions were reversed and he was forced to accept help, he'd probably feel the same. "What are you making?"

"Spaghetti and meatballs, garlic bread and peas. That's something everyone can agree on. Well the spaghetti and bread anyway. The peas will be a battle."

"I wasn't a fan of vegetables as a kid either."

"They used to eat them. Now..." Her voice hitched. "Now they're changing. I understand the reason they're acting out, but it's not making my life any easier."

He didn't know what to say. Roz's illness really was taking a toll on all of them.

"And school starts in about a month. I'm not sure whether that will make life better or worse."

"It's hard to know. We'll just have to do our best to support them. Remember, you aren't alone. I'm not here just to do laundry and cut grass. I'm here for the emotional stuff, too."

She blinked rapidly, as if keeping tears at bay. He hoped she was successful. Her tears cut him to his core. He was discovering that when she hurt, he hurt. "Thanks."

"I know you can cook dinner by yourself. Do you mind if I keep you company?"

"I'd like that."

They talked about inconsequential matters, but he felt as if they were communicating in a way they hadn't since he'd arrived. When he heard the kids' voices floating through the open windows and the sound of their feet pounding on the front porch, he let them in. Nathaniel was holding a gigantic bouquet of flowers.

"Wow," Paul said. "Where did you get those?"

"Miss Camille helped us pick them," Megan said. "They're for Mommy."

"Who's Miss Camille?"

"She lives at the ranch."

"Your mom's going to love them," Paul said.

"Where is Mommy?" Suzanne asked.

"I'm in here," Roz called.

Paul followed the children into the kitchen. Although Roz had started to wilt while they'd been talking, she perked up when she saw the kids.

"My goodness. Where did you get those flowers?"

"We picked them," Megan said. "Do you like them?"

"I love them."

Suzanne and Megan each held a plate filled with treats. "We have cookies and cake, too."

"Wonderful. We can have some for dessert. Now wash your hands and let's have dinner. I want to hear all about your day."

There was commotion as the kids ran into the powder room to wash their hands and Roz began to put the food on the table.

"Where do you want these?" Paul asked, picking up the vase Nathaniel had set on the table.

"How about on my dresser?"

He nodded. When he reached her closed door, he hesitated before opening it. Although he'd been inside her room on several occasions since he and the kids had helped her change rooms, it felt strange to step into her private space when she wasn't in there. After placing the bouquet where she would be able to see it from her bed, he returned to the kitchen.

Everyone was sitting down, so he quickly took his seat. Once they'd blessed the food, everyone dug in. As expected, Nathaniel and Megan chattered about the great time they'd had riding the horses. Suzanne confessed that she'd been scared of the big animals, then began to talk about playing with the rancher's dog. It was the most Suzanne had talked in weeks. Roz was smiling broadly, and Paul noticed that she'd eaten more than she had in quite a while. It still wasn't as much as he would have liked, but it was an improvement.

After they'd eaten and each kid had chosen the dessert they wanted, they continued to talk about their day for twenty more minutes. When Suzanne's head began to bob, Paul suggested that the kids take their baths and then read or watch television until bedtime. He'd expected some pushback, but the kids nodded and headed upstairs. He followed and filled the tub for the girls. When he returned to the kitchen, Roz was gone. He heard her moving around in her room and realized she was just as worn-out as her kids. Still, no matter how tired she was, he knew she was happy. That made him happy, too. And wasn't that an unsettling thought?

Chapter Four

Roz read the number on the phone's caller ID and grimaced. It was the school. Though school had only started three weeks ago, it had been rough going for Suzanne. Suzanne had clung to her before Paul hustled the kids out of the house that morning, so Roz wasn't entirely surprised by the call. Still, Roz had hoped that Suzanne would be better once she was in class.

Suzanne used to love school. She'd always been the first person awake and dressed, sitting at the breakfast table every morning. Last year, when she'd been in kindergarten and still learning the days of the week, she'd often been ready to go on Saturdays.

She had a wonderful teacher and all of her friends from kindergarten were in her class. Despite that, Suzanne was not enjoying first grade. According to her teacher, Mr. Reed, Suzanne was becoming more withdrawn each day. She didn't answer questions in class, nor did she play with her friends at recess. Instead, she sat alone on a swing, twisting her foot in the ground.

Roz had made the school staff aware of her health challenges and they agreed that Roz's illness was probably the reason for Suzanne's behavior. Although they'd been working together, they hadn't figured out a way to help her.

"Ms. Martin."

Roz sighed upon hearing the principal's voice. "Yes."

"I'm calling about Suzanne. She's having a rough day. Are you able to come to the school this morning?"

"Of course." After setting a time, Roz hung up and stared at the phone. She was running out of ideas, but she still had plenty of hope.

"What's up?" Paul asked, coming into the front room. Now that the kids were in school, he used the kitchen as his office and spent most of the day working there. She'd gotten used to the piles of paper and the two computers he used, but she still hadn't quite gotten used to seeing him day and night. Dressed casually in jeans and a T-shirt, he looked so good she couldn't help but stare.

"That was the school. They want me to come in to discuss Suzanne." She blew out a breath and adjusted the scarf covering her head. All of her hair had fallen out and she was completely bald. "I need to get going. I told the principal I'd be there in twenty minutes."

Paul grabbed his keys. "I'll drive."

"You don't have to come. I feel good enough to drive." It had been a week since her last chemo treatment. Though feeling good was a distant memory and often seemed like a fantasy she'd created, she was feeling okay, all things considered. Just knowing that she'd be having surgery once all of the chemo was out of her system, gave her hope that she would soon be feeling like her old self. "Besides, this is your work time. I feel guilty enough for disrupting your life as much as I have."

His eyes narrowed as he stared at her. "Stop apologizing for upsetting my life. Yes, you asked for my help, but I could have said no. I chose to come to Sweet Briar. And I'm choosing to stay. If I wanted to leave, I would be gone and nothing you said or did could stop me. Suzanne is in trouble. We both can see that. And it's going to take both of us to help her."

Relief flooded her. She wasn't alone. She didn't have to handle this by herself. "Thank you."

"We're family. And families take care of each other."

Family. She could remember a time not that long ago when he'd come right out and said they weren't family. She and Paul had come a long way.

"Thank you. I appreciate it."

The ride to the school took fifteen minutes, but it seemed longer. Worry about Suzanne was only part of the reason time stretched. The other was sitting beside her, his strong hands confidently gripping the steering wheel. Once more, Roz reminded herself that what she and Paul had shared had gone up in flames, leaving only the ashes of bitterness behind. Sitting so close to him that the warmth from his body drove her chills away, she was tempted to fantasize about regaining what they'd once had. But she swatted the imaginings away. She was a realist who recognized the impossible when it smacked her in the face.

As Paul pulled into the parking lot and switched off the car, Roz cleared her mind of everything but her daughter. Suzanne needed a focused, present mother, not one living in a dreamworld where fairy tales came true. Paul held out his hand as they walked into the school and she took it without a second thought. She wouldn't reject his support when she needed it most.

They checked in with the school secretary, who led them to the principal's office. Mr. Reed and Ms.

Hawkins, the school psychologist, were also present, sitting side by side at the round table.

"Ms. Martin." The principal stood as he greeted her.

"Mr. Bennett." She nodded to the other people. "This is Paul Stephens, Suzanne's uncle."

"Please have a seat," Mr. Bennett said, indicating two empty chairs. Paul pulled out a chair for Roz, then sat. Their chairs were so close together that their arms brushed. Though it had no business doing so, her rebellious heart skipped a beat at the casual contact.

"We're concerned about Suzanne," Ms. Hawkins said, getting directly to the point. Roz had met with the other woman before, and while Roz was impressed by Ms. Hawkins's competence, she found the other woman a bit brusque. She was no-nonsense, from the top of her no-frills hairstyle down to the tips of her sensible pumps. But Roz didn't care that the psychologist dressed as if she were in her fifties instead of her twenties, as long as she could help Suzanne.

"We are, too," Roz said.

"Of course you are," Mr. Reed added, his tone soothing. No wonder the kids all adored him. He might be built like a Mack truck, but he was a big cuddly teddy bear.

"We all need to work together to help Suzanne," Paul added. "Since you have expertise, we're eager to listen to any suggestions you have. Hopefully, you'll have ideas that we haven't considered."

Ms. Hawkins nodded her head as if surprised by Paul's attitude, making Roz wonder just what the other woman had expected. The counselor picked up a file and flipped through several pages. "Mr. Reed recently requested that I visit his classroom. I've spent several hours observing Suzanne over the past week. She cries easily. The other children and Mr. Reed try to comfort her, but she's become more disconsolate with every passing day. She's definitely different from the happy child she was last year."

Roz's eyes filled with tears at the thought of her baby being in such pain. She didn't know a tear had escaped until she felt a tissue being pressed into her hand. She flashed a grateful look at Paul as she wiped the dampness from her face. Crying was not going to help her little girl.

"Do you have any suggestions?" Roz asked. "We're trying everything we know, but we'd appreciate your help."

"Actually, I do," Ms. Hawkins replied. "Suzanne is worried about you, of course. But she's also worried about herself. She doesn't know what will happen to her if you're no longer here. She's afraid her family is going to disintegrate and she'll be left alone. You need to show her that her family is strong. Eat meals together, play games and watch movies together."

"We already do that," Roz said.

"Good. Keep it up." The counselor looked first at Roz and then at Paul. "And of course, the less tension there is, the better off she'll be."

Although Ms. Hawkins didn't come out and say it, Roz wondered if Suzanne had sensed the tension between her and Paul and mentioned it to the counselor. That would explain her surprised expression earlier.

"There are several activities underway in Sweet Briar and more scheduled in the upcoming weeks. I'm aware of your health challenges, Ms. Martin, but if you're able to participate, they're worth considering."

Ms. Hawkins flipped through her file once more, and this time she pulled out a typed piece of paper and handed it over. She also gathered several colorful brochures. "I've taken the liberty of getting information on activities that might appeal to you and your family. Not all of them are in Sweet Briar, but it gives you a lot to choose from. A few happy family occasions will definitely help. Of course, all the excursions in the world won't work miracles, but they can help to lower her stress."

"Thank you for your help," Roz said. "I'm grateful for all the people in Suzanne's life who care about her."

Ms. Hawkins smiled. "She's a wonderful girl. Together we can help her work through her emotions and reach a happy place. I'll be meeting with her on a regular basis. But don't set your expectations too high. This will take more than a couple of weeks. Suzanne is experiencing feelings she doesn't understand and can't explain. She's confused and frightened."

As Roz listened to the counselor, she stiffened her spine. She needed to be strong for her child. For all of her children. Because even if Nathaniel and Megan weren't displaying the same signs as Suzanne, she knew her illness affected them, as well.

After thanking everyone for their concern and help, Roz and Paul walked to the car without speaking. Roz didn't know what to say and imagined Paul had the same problem. She glanced over the typed list of activities and flipped through the brochures as Paul drove home.

"Anything look good?" Paul asked as he pulled onto their block.

"A couple of things sound interesting."

"Do you think you're going to be up to it?"

"I'm going to have to be."

"That's not how this works, Roz. You can't will yourself to be physically strong."

"I love my daughter, and I'm going to do what's necessary to get her through this."

"Love isn't some magical cure. Love won't heal your cancer or stop the effects of the chemo. Heck, as much as you and the kids love each other, if love was enough, you'd be well by now. In fact, you'd never have gotten sick in the first place."

She sucked in a breath, prepared to argue, then stopped. Paul was right. Love might make her feel better emotionally, but, sadly, it didn't do a thing for her physically.

Paul turned off the car then placed his hand over hers. The heat from his fingers warmed the chill that had seeped into her bones, growing colder with each of Ms. Hawkins's words until Roz was frozen inside. "You aren't alone. I'm here."

"For how long?"

"As long as it takes." His thumb moved over her hand in a gentle caress. A few seconds later, he frowned and snatched his hand away.

She blew out a breath. "I don't think this is going to work. You can't put the past behind you. When you find yourself being nice to me, giving me a little bit of comfort, you pull away. It's like you're reminding yourself that I'm a horrible person. Sometimes I feel like you're replaying every mistake I've ever made in your mind so you don't have to consider the fact that I might have changed. It would be okay if it was just me, but it's not. Suzanne has picked up on it. She's already stressed out. She doesn't need our flawed relationship adding to her stress."

Roz got out of the car and then slammed the door behind her. It might have been childish, but it felt good.

* * *

Paul watched as Roz stormed up the stairs. She was totally wrong. He hadn't been thinking about how badly she'd treated him in the past. Feeling her soft skin beneath his fingers had stirred up happy memories of the times they'd spent together. From the moment they'd met in chemistry class, they'd been at ease with each other. They'd shared the same offbeat sense of humor and had laughed together at the silliest things. Roz had possessed the unique ability to not only find pleasure in the simplest things but to help him find that same joy, as well.

The memories had been accompanied by a hint of desire that was completely inappropriate. Given the radio silence between him and Kristin, he could safely say that that relationship was over. But maybe a reconciliation wasn't out of the question. And even though he was willing to forgive Roz for the past, only a fool traveled the same road twice. And he wasn't a fool. So, no matter how pleasant the reminiscences, he wouldn't allow them to blind him. He wasn't going to open his heart to her again.

He climbed out of the car and followed Roz into the house. He found her in the kitchen. A pot of water was on the stove and the pungent aroma of vinegar filled the air. She was snatching items from the cabinet with swift, angry movements, arranging them on the kitchen table. Clearly, she was about to cook something. From the look of things, it was going to be a lot of work. Just what she didn't need to be doing. She needed to rest.

One thing he knew about Roz: she was stubborn as all get-out. He considered suggesting that she turn off the stove and lie down for a while, but he knew if he did, she'd turn him into the bad guy.

"What are you making?" He was pleased to note his voice contained the friendly curiosity he was aiming for.

She put a hand on her hip and narrowed her eyes. Apparently, she wasn't fooled. "Caramel apples. Why?"

He smiled. He loved taffy apples. It had been years since he'd had one. And that one had been a mass-produced apple he'd bought at the grocery store. Roz's homemade caramel apple was going to taste a hundred times better. His mouth watered at the thought.

"Want help?" This time his friendly tone was sincere.

Her chest rose and fell as she took a long, deep breath, signaling that a definite no was on its way out of her lips. "To be honest—"

He cut her off before she could continue. "We need to provide a stress-free home for Suzanne, remember? Which means we need to work on our relationship. What better way to work out the bugs than by cooking together?" He held out his hand. "So...friends?"

She paused, then shook his hand. “Friends.”

“And can I help?”

“Fine. You can help.”

He washed his hands, then pointed at the pot. “What’s that for?”

“To remove the wax from the apples. A couple of seconds in the solution does the trick.”

“There are some apple orchards not too far from here. Maybe we can add apple picking to the list.”

“Maybe.”

She sounded a bit noncommittal, but he let it pass. No doubt she was adjusting to their new, minutes-old friendship, as was he. Plus, she had the added burden of determining if she felt strong enough for something so physical.

He knew she still experienced episodes of fatigue. The doctor couldn’t predict how long the bouts would last. Could be weeks, could be months. Frustrated with the doctor’s answer, Paul had consulted his friend, and the town doctor, Rick Tyler. Rick had pretty much given the same nonanswer. The best guidance Rick could offer was for Paul to make sure Roz ate well and rested often. And, of course, she needed to keep her stress level down. Another reason for Paul to adjust his attitude.

“What should I do now?” he asked.

“You can put the sticks into the apples.”

“What are you going to do?”

“I’m going to mix the ingredients for the caramel.”

He pictured her standing over the hot stove, stirring the mixture. No way. "How about we switch jobs?"

"Paul, I'm not an invalid."

"And I'm not a child. That's something you would have Suzanne do. I'm a man. I can do more than shove a stick into an apple."

"Fine. You can make the caramel. But don't let it burn."

"I think I can handle that. How hard can it be?"

Thirty minutes later, Paul slid the tray of caramel-covered apples into the refrigerator, then let out a loud sigh. Making caramel sauce had sounded so easy. And it probably was if you knew what you were doing. He didn't. Stirring and keeping an eye on the candy thermometer, making sure the caramel didn't get too hot, then pouring everything into a metal bowl and watching the thermometer again so the caramel didn't get too cold was nerve-racking. Maybe he should be the one with his feet up, nursing a cup of broccoli cheddar soup that Brandon Danielson, owner of Heaven on Earth, Sweet Briar's very popular restaurant, dropped off yesterday.

If he was going to be honest with himself—and why the heck wouldn't he?—it was being alone in close confines with Roz that had him sweating. Sitting at the table, illuminated by the sunlight that streamed through the window and looking angelic, she awakened emotions in him he'd fought to keep dormant. Yet he found himself unable to stem the tide of softer feelings flowing through him. He was struggling to crush the need to make everything better for her. This was a battle he couldn't lose if he expected to walk away with his heart intact.

She looked up and caught him staring at her. He reflexively started to turn away but caught himself just in time. If they were going to lower the tension in this house, he needed to treat her as a friend, so he smiled and crossed the room, dropping into a chair across from her. "You could have told me how intense that would be."

She laughed and her eyes lit up. His heart thumped against his rib cage in response. "You're the one who insisted on a man-size job."

"True, true." Despite his burned finger, he felt pretty good. "Do you think the kids will like them?"

"Oh, yeah. They love sweet things."

His eyes shot to her full lips. So did he. And that was the problem.

Chapter Five

"I don't want to eat my peas. I want a taffy apple now," Suzanne said, her bottom lip quivering. A tear slipped from her eye and slid down her chubby cheek, breaking Paul's heart. The kids knew dessert came after dinner, but that didn't make seeing Suzanne in tears any easier. He knew she wasn't upset simply because she wanted to eat her treat, but rather because of everything happening in her life. Roz's illness and the fear of losing her mother weighed on Suzanne's mind, and she was handling it the only way she knew how—by acting out.

Roz eased from her chair and knelt beside Suzanne, taking her daughter's hands into her own.

"I know you must be disappointed. I would be, too. But we always finish our dinner before we eat dessert. You know that."

"But my tummy is running out of room. If I eat my peas I won't have any space for my taffy apple. And everybody else will get to eat theirs. It's not fair."

"I see. Well, how about this? I won't eat my taffy apple until you have room in your tummy. Will that make you feel better?"

Suzanne nodded.

"I won't eat mine either." Paul said. He shot a meaningful glance at the other children who let out heavy sighs.

Nathaniel had lifted his apple to his mouth, but now lowered it without biting it. "I guess I can wait, too. Can I watch TV now?"

"Sure," Paul said. "Put your plate in the sink."

"Me, too?" Megan asked, grabbing her empty plate before jumping up to follow her brother.

Paul nodded.

"Come on. No more crying. Let's finish those peas." Roz wiped Suzanne's face. The little girl stiffened. She looked terrified and guilty. "What's wrong?"

"I didn't mean to cry, Mommy. I tried not to, but it just came out."

"That's okay. I understand."

"Gabby's sister said when kids cry in front of their

mommies that their mommies' hearts break. I don't want you to have a breaked heart. You can die with a breaked heart."

Paul met Roz's gaze as she pulled Suzanne into her arms. The pain in Roz's eyes was enough to break his heart. "That's not what it means. When a heart is broken you don't die. It just means you're sad."

"Are you sure?" Suzanne asked. "Gabby's sister is big. She's even bigger than Nathaniel."

"I'm very sure."

"Okay," Suzanne whispered, a trace of doubt lingering in her voice. "I don't want you to die, Mommy."

"I won't." Roz held her daughter, then brushed a tear from her own eye. Paul discovered he needed to do the same. He'd been around Suzanne for months. How could he not have noticed how much pain and fear she'd been holding inside? A feeling of helplessness threatened to consume him, but he pushed it aside. This was not the time to give up. The battle to help Suzanne might be tough, but so was he.

Crossing the room, he wrapped his arm around Roz and Suzanne in a brief hug before helping Roz to stand. He'd been fighting to remain immune to her, but he was rapidly losing that battle. Seeing Roz's pain was like having his heart ripped from his chest.

"Let's finish those peas so you can get to your treat," he said. "I worked hard on these apples."

Suzanne looked at him in surprise. "You made the taffy apples, Uncle Paul?"

"I sure did." He looked at Roz and winked. "With a little help from your mommy."

"You did them together? At the same time?"

"We did."

Suzanne looked at her mother for confirmation. When Roz nodded, Suzanne's mouth lifted into a tiny smile. "I know they'll be double good."

Suzanne polished off her peas, set her plate in the sink then raced from the room, leaving Roz and Paul alone. Once Suzanne was gone, Roz's forced smile slipped and she looked like she'd been punched in the gut. He knew the feeling.

"I didn't know she was worried about that." Roz slumped and dropped her head onto her folded arms. His heart still aching, he circled the table and wrapped his arm around her shaking shoulders.

"Don't cry."

"You don't understand." She lifted her tearstained face to him. "Do you have any idea how many times I told her that seeing her cry broke my heart? How many times I've said that to all three of my children? Who knows what Megan and Nathaniel are thinking? For all I know, they're worried about the same thing and just haven't said anything."

"I don't think they are. Neither of them is as literal as Suzanne. But if it makes you feel better, we can ask them."

"My kids are hurting and it's all my fault."

"How is any of this your fault? You didn't try to get cancer. That's something that happened to you. And you certainly aren't responsible for what some kid tells your daughter about hearts breaking." He reached out and cupped her damp face then wiped away the tears. "And you most certainly aren't to blame for the tension that Suzanne sensed. The blame for that lies squarely on my shoulders."

"You came when I needed you, Paul."

She may be willing to let him off the hook with a simple apology, but he wasn't. "And I made a mess of everything."

"No, you didn't. You kept my kids fed, in clean clothes and safe. That's what matters. Besides, we agreed to leave the past and all its mistakes behind us. So let's start over from today and do what we can to help the kids. All I want is for them to be happy and healthy."

Was it? Could she really be happy with so little? She was still a young woman. Certainly she would want to fall in love and marry again. Not that her romantic life was any of his business. He was here to help with her physical concerns and her children. So why was he having a hard time remembering that?

Roz put down the last brochure, adding it to the small pile of activities to be considered. The ferry tour sounded interesting and not too strenuous. And she loved the water. She knew that the bouts with fatigue could continue for a while, but she wouldn't let the lack of energy control her life. If she did, she might start to feel sorry for herself. Aunt Rosemary had frequently reminded Roz that so many people had it much worse and that it would be considered ungrateful to do anything other than count her blessings.

Roz's aunt had pointed out numerous times how Roz could have been with her parents when the accident occurred. That after her parents' deaths she could have been left with no one to care for her. Aunt Rosemary had regularly pointed out that she hadn't shied away from the responsibility thrust upon her. But Roz had never wanted to be an obligation. She'd wanted to be loved. Cherished. And here she was, once more an obligation to someone who didn't love her.

Her eyes stung with unshed tears that she wouldn't let fall. Being an obligation was bad enough, but she would suffer through that. What she wouldn't do was become an object of pity. She'd seen pity in Paul's eyes when she'd broken down in the kitchen. She'd wanted to jerk away from his hand, but his gentle touch had left her paralyzed.

She forced herself to face the truth. She hadn't wanted to move. She'd dreamed of that type of interaction for a long time. She'd wanted him to touch her in a way that wasn't purely clinical. Sometimes she felt like her illness had taken away all of her sex appeal, that cancer had removed all that was feminine in her, leaving behind the shell of the woman she'd once been.

When she'd finally felt his hands on her, she'd wanted to lean against him and breathe him in until all of her troubles faded away. That would have been a mistake, so she'd made herself pull away. She wasn't going to get reality tangled up with her hopes and wishes. Life wasn't a fairy tale. She didn't have a fairy godmother who could fix Roz's life with the wave of a magic wand. Paul wasn't going to magically fall in love with her. They weren't going to live happily ever after.

She blew out a pent-up breath and stood. Stressful days often made it hard for her to sleep. One thing that never failed to relax her was a nice bubble bath followed by a mug of chamomile tea. Since she'd been ill, she'd settled for quick baths and even quicker showers. Tonight she was going to pamper herself.

She grabbed her phone and turned on her playlist, letting her favorite classical piano solos fill the air. Next, she placed candles around the bathroom and lit them. As she filled the tub, she added her favorite rose bath oil. She inhaled the scent and the tension began to melt from her body. She stripped quickly, then sank into the warm water, sliding down until she was nearly submerged. Blowing out a breath, she let the flickering candlelight, the soothing music and the sweet aroma of roses transport her to a happier place and time. A time when all was right in her world. Of course, that time was mostly a figment of her imagination, but right now she didn't care.

Roz soaked until the water cooled, then quickly washed up. It wasn't until she was wrapped in a towel that she realized she hadn't brought a stitch of clothing into the bathroom. She'd been so eager to escape her worries that she'd left her robe hanging on a hook on her bedroom door. For a fleeting second, she considered grabbing her dirty clothes from the hamper and putting them on again, but what sense did that make?

And who was she hiding from? The kids were asleep and Paul was in his room. And if he came out? So what? What would it matter? He practically looked through her anyway. He'd made it plain from day one that she'd killed any romantic feelings he'd had for her. Besides, he had no reason to come out of his room. She opened the bathroom door, stepped into the hallway and bumped right into him.

"Roz." His voice was low and raspy, sending shivers down her spine. His eyes skimmed her body, making her realize just how small the light blue terry cloth rectangle actually was. She wasn't very tall, but the towel wasn't very big and hit her midthigh, revealing most of her legs.

Finally, his eyes returned to hers. The sense of

relief she'd felt fled at the heat and longing she saw there. Her heart began to pound and she stepped back. He blinked and the heat in his eyes fizzled out.

"You're awake," she said, blurting out the first thing that came to mind, no matter how inane.

"I was about to take a shower. I didn't realize you were still in the bathroom."

That was the problem with old houses. They only had one full bathroom. Paul had talked about expanding the main floor powder room, but she'd turned him down. He'd done enough by creating a first-floor bedroom. Standing here wrapped in a towel, she wished she'd taken him up on the offer.

"I'm finished now." She told her feet to move so he could step into the bathroom, but her body wasn't inclined to listen to her.

"I see." He didn't walk around her. Perhaps his body was just as rebellious as hers.

That thought made her smile. And he smiled in return. She unfroze and stepped to her right. He moved at the same time, but to his left, and once more they blocked each other. They sidestepped again, as if they were dancing to silent music. He stopped, placing a hand on her bare shoulder. His touch was gentle yet it was powerful enough to weaken her knees.

Roz nibbled on her bottom lip, doing her best to keep from moaning. She wanted to reach out and touch him, if only for a second. If she had the nerve, she'd stand on her tiptoes and brush her lips against his. Of course, she wouldn't. There was enough tension between them already. She didn't need to add more by being reckless and impetuous. Exhaling deeply, she moved to the right then shook her head as he moved to his left at the same time.

"At this rate, we'll be here all night." He took two steps back and to the side, allowing her to pass.

"Thanks," she mumbled as she scrambled past him, then walked as sedately as she could down the stairs and to her room. Once there, she closed her door and leaned against it. Whew. That was awkward and something else. Hot. She knew that Paul had experienced the same burning desire as she had, if only for a moment. Not that either of them would ever act on it. There might be desire between them, but there was no trust. Once trust was broken, it was nearly impossible to get back. And there couldn't be a relationship without trust.

Paul stepped into the bathroom, then blew out a shaky breath. He closed his eyes, but he could still see the image of Roz wrapped in that pale blue towel, the scrap of fabric tucked between her perky breasts. That sight would be forever emblazoned in his mind. He wouldn't forget how sexy she looked as long as he lived. There'd been a drop of water on her shoulder, and it had taken every ounce of his self-control to not lick it off her soft skin. He hadn't planned to touch her, but with one glance at her, rational thought had flown, and he'd felt like he'd die if he didn't.

He inhaled and his lungs were instantly filled with the scent of roses. The sweet scent of Roz. Ever since he'd come to stay with her, he'd been aware of the floral fragrance that was as much a part of her as her brown eyes.

Now he knew it was the result of something she put in her bath or splashed on her body. He should open the window and let in fresh air until no hint of roses remained. That's what a smart man would do. Instead, he inhaled again, savoring the perfumed air. Eyes still closed, he let his mind drift back to a few moments ago and the wonderful vision of Roz wrapped in that towel. Frowning, he shut off the thought before it could go too far. He couldn't let himself get swept away by her beauty, no matter how desperately he wanted to take her into his arms. That would be a mistake. And he was through making mistakes with Roz.

But how could he be sure it was a mistake? He'd been so sure he was over her and that he would never want anything to do with her. Now he caught himself thinking of her at the most inopportune times. It was becoming harder to resist her appeal. The more time he spent with her, the more she occupied his thoughts.

He shook his head. So what if he was thinking of her. That was probably the result of living in such close quarters. Once she was well and he returned to his regular life, he'd forget all about her again and these unwanted feelings would go back to wherever they came from.

At least that's what he hoped.

Chapter Six

"You ready for this?" Paul asked.

Roz nodded. She'd woken up this morning feeling happy and energized. And though she didn't feel as good as she used to, today was a good day. Excitement buzzed through her veins like ginger ale, sweet and clear and fizzy.

"Great." He placed the platter of sausages on the middle of the kitchen table, then called the kids in for breakfast.

"I don't want to eat now," Megan complained as she pulled out her chair. "I want to finish coloring my picture."

"You can color later," Roz said, putting a waffle on a plate and setting it before her daughter.

"I'm going to be in the clean plate club," Suzanne said, "because I don't want to make your heart break, Mommy."

Roz brushed a hand over Suzanne's hair then tugged her braid. "My heart won't break if you don't eat everything. But your stomach will be hungry. And noisy."

"I'm always ready to eat," Nathaniel said, taking his seat.

"Me, too," Paul said, putting a platter of scrambled eggs on the table. They didn't ordinarily eat such big breakfasts, but they were going to need fuel for today's adventure.

After everyone started to eat, Paul shot her a look. They'd decided to wait until after breakfast to tell the kids about the ferry ride, but from the excited expression on his face, Paul wasn't going to be able to stick to the plan. He looked like he might burst any second.

"Go ahead," she said.

"You don't want to be the one to tell them?"

"You can do it." It thrilled her to see how eager he was to take the kids on this outing. With everything that had happened, they hadn't gone on any family trips this past year. The kids had gone on field trips with the youth center together, but this was the first time she and Paul were taking them on a family outing. They weren't a traditional family, of course. Paul wasn't their father. But he was their uncle and they loved each other.

"Tell us what?" Nathaniel asked, using a piece of his waffle to sop up the syrup on his plate.

"Yeah, what?" Megan asked, pausing before scooping eggs into her mouth.

Roz noticed that Suzanne didn't look up or appear the slightest bit interested in the conversation. She was eating with a determination that struck fear in Roz's heart. Suzanne was too afraid of upsetting Roz. Her little girl was well and truly breaking her heart.

"We're going on a ferry ride," Paul answered.

That caught Suzanne's attention and her head snapped up. "I like fairies. They're pretty. The tooth fairy puts money under your pillow when your tooth falls out. Megan got a dollar a few times. None of my teeth fell out yet."

"You'll lose a tooth soon," Roz promised.

"Will I get a dollar?"

"Yes. But it's not that kind of fairy. This kind of ferry is a boat."

"We're going on a boat ride?" Nathaniel asked, his eyes gleaming with anticipation. "Are we going fishing?"

"No. But we might see some dolphins and maybe some wild horses," Paul said.

"Horses in the water?" Megan asked. "Horses don't swim."

"Maybe they're seahorses," Nathaniel joked.

Paul chuckled and goose bumps popped up on Roz's arms at the sound that once had been a regular part of her life. Now it was an all too rare occurrence. "We're going to an island. The horses will be there."

"I love horses." Nathaniel grinned. "Are we going to ride them?"

"No. Just look at them. And we might pick up some sand dollars."

"They make money out of sand?" Megan asked.

Roz and Paul laughed and their eyes met briefly. Paul looked away, severing the connection. She suppressed a sigh.

"Not exactly," Paul said. "Now, who wants to go?"

"We're all going?" Suzanne asked cautiously. She looked around the table and her eyes landed first on Paul, then on Roz.

"Yes."

Suzanne pondered that and her little body relaxed. She smiled. "I want to go."

"Then let's finish eating."

After that, there was lots of laughter and commotion as the kids got dressed.

"Depending on the speed and the wind, boat rides can get pretty wet, so, to be on the safe side, we should bring extra clothes and leave them in the car," Paul said.

"Have you been on a lot of boat rides?" Nathaniel asked.

He grinned. "I own a boat, so yeah, I've been on boat rides."

"You have your own boat, Uncle Paul? Why don't we ever go out on it?"

"It's docked in Florida, where I live. Maybe I can take you out sometime."

"That would be awesome."

As Roz listened to the conversation, she made a mental note to tell Paul not to make promises he wouldn't keep. When he returned to Florida, she and the kids would be out of his mind as surely as they'd be out of his sight. Being left behind hurt like heck and was a pain she wanted her kids to avoid. She didn't want them hoping for a call that wouldn't come.

After everyone was securely seat-belted in the Mercedes SUV, Paul steered the car down the road. Roz turned the radio to a smooth jazz station. Past experience had taught her that the mellow sounds quieted the children on long car rides better than her frequent admonitions to use inside voices. That and making sure the kids didn't sit close enough to actually touch. They each guarded their personal car space fiercely. By the time the second song ended, the children had settled down. Megan and Suzanne, seated in the second row, were playing with their dolls. Nathaniel, sitting in the third row, was peppering Paul with questions about his boat.

As they drove down the highway, Roz watched

the passing scenery and let her mind float away on the clouds. Today she would simply let events occur. She wouldn't waste a minute worrying about the future or regretting the past. She would be present in the moment and enjoy everything, making new happy memories.

The salty smell of the ocean began to filter through the open windows and the kids stirred with anticipation. They'd spent many days playing at the beach in Sweet Briar, but they'd never ridden in a boat. For a fleeting moment, she forgot her vow to let the day just happen and slipped into worry mode. What if the kids didn't like it? What if one of them got seasick?

"Don't fret," Paul said, reaching across the console between the seats and giving her hand a gentle squeeze. "We're going to have the best time ever."

That simple phrase transported her to a time when she and Paul had been young and so much in love. Losing her parents at a young age and being raised by someone who hadn't wanted her had left Roz insecure. A part of her couldn't believe that Paul actually loved her. He'd been the football hero and she'd been the orphan girl whose cheap clothes were never in style. Every day, no matter what they did, he'd always promised that they were going to have the best time ever. And she always had.

Now she wondered if the words held the same significance for him as they did for her. She shook her head. Doubtful. Over the years, he'd probably said the same thing to countless women.

"You don't believe me?" Paul asked. "You used to."

"I believe you. It's just that mother worry."

He grinned confidently. "Don't worry. They're going to love it."

Suzanne leaned over from her seat behind Paul, pulling her thumb from her mouth. "You're holding Mommy's hand."

"Yes. Is that okay?"

Suzanne nodded, wiped her thumb on her pants and then began brushing her doll's hair.

Paul caught Roz's eye and winked. Oh, what she wouldn't give to know what that meant.

Paul parked, helped the girls and Roz from the car and then led the way to the ticket booth. He'd made reservations in advance, so he handed over the cash and took the tickets. Although he moved with confidence, his mind was a whirl of confusion. Why in the world had he held Roz's hand? Sure, his initial intention had been to offer assurance. But that wouldn't have taken more than the briefest contact. Once he'd felt Roz's warm skin beneath his hand, he couldn't let go to save his life. Instead, he'd turned over her hand and pressed their palms together. It had felt so good to hold her hand. So right. Being with her felt right.

Which only proved what a gullible fool he was, because he should know that nothing with Roz was right.

"Which boat is ours?" Megan asked as she placed her small hand into his. She smiled up at him, trust on her young face. No matter his mixed-up feelings for Roz, he was clear about one thing: he absolutely loved her kids.

Nathaniel was maturing into a nice young man. Paul was proud of the way he looked after his sisters and mother, but he worried that Nathaniel attempted to carry too much responsibility on his shoulders. Paul was doing his best to share the burden and allow Nathaniel to be a boy. But Paul would be leaving and Nathaniel would once again try to assume the role of man of the house.

Paul glanced at Roz. Dressed in faded jeans and a long-sleeved purple T-shirt, with a purple floral scarf wrapped around her head, she looked very appealing. There was nothing especially sexy about her clothes. In fact, the jeans were a little bit loose, hinting at her curves instead of showing them off. Despite that, she was much too sexy for his peace of mind.

But it was her face that was most irresistible. Her brown skin was clear and her eyes danced with excitement. Suzanne said something that made her laugh and the sound sneaked past his walls, squeezing his heart until it hurt. He didn't want her awakening his emotions and exhuming the feelings he'd buried long ago. But he couldn't keep her at arm's length if they were going to eliminate the tension between them. And Suzanne needed the tension to be gone. Truth be told, he'd prefer living in a stress-free home, too.

"Yeah, Uncle Paul," Nathaniel said, wandering back to them, "which boat is ours?"

There were only four boats in sight and he easily spotted theirs. He pointed at a midsize vessel that could hold twenty passengers. "That's it right there."

Nathaniel raced down the wooden pier, his sisters following behind, calling for him to wait for them. Paul paused, waiting until Roz reached his side, then reached out and grabbed her hand. Telling himself that he wasn't holding her hand because he wanted to feel connected to her again, but rather because he wanted to appear friendly in case Suzanne looked back, he glanced down at her. "You still feel okay?"

Her lips lifted in a sweet smile. "Yes. It feels good to be doing something out of the ordinary. Something fun. These past few months have been pretty harsh. Not that I'm complaining," she added quickly. "I'm thankful that I'm getting better."

He gave her hand a gentle tug. "No one would ever accuse you of complaining. You're the most positive person I know."

"It's hard. Sometimes I just want to cry my eyes out."

"Sometimes you do cry your eyes out."

She gasped and stopped walking.

"The walls in your house are really thin, Roz."

"But you sleep upstairs."

"Don't you think I come downstairs to check on you?"

Her bottom lip trembled, and he felt like a jerk. Obviously, she didn't want him knowing she was afraid. Did she really believe he didn't know that? Or did she think he didn't care enough to make sure she had everything she needed? He knew that he'd been distant—that had been deliberate on his part. But he hadn't considered how badly his actions had hurt her. It finally hit him just how alone Roz must have felt—and must still feel—even with him there.

His stomach churned as he thought about how he'd allowed Roz to suffer silently. She must think he didn't care a whit about her. And why wouldn't she? He'd acted that way. Worse, he'd told her that. Reaching out, he touched her cheek. "I'm sorry, Roz."

"You don't need to apologize. I asked you to help me care for my kids and you did. That's all that matters."

He started to argue, but the kids began calling them. "We'll finish this conversation later," he promised.

"There's nothing to finish," she said.

There was most definitely something to finish. He just wasn't certain what it was.

Chapter Seven

Roz lifted her head into the wind. A light spray of water blew on her face as the boat knifed through the waves, but she didn't think it unpleasant. In fact, she found it exhilarating. This was turning into a great day.

The kids were sitting on the bench between her and Paul, chattering a mile a minute. Even Suzanne commented now and again, although she still was quieter than Roz liked. Roz knew she shouldn't expect a miracle, but she still hoped for one. Suzanne had withdrawn gradually, so it was going to take time for her to become her old self. Even so, Roz found herself watching her daughter, hoping to catch glimpses of her happy child.

Roz turned her attention back to the ship's captain, who'd gone from extolling the virtues of the ship to delivering interesting tidbits about the surroundings. The girls had listened for a while, then, growing bored, began trying to catch water on their tongues. The captain steered the boat to a pier and the kids jumped to their feet.

"Hold on. Wait until we're parked," Roz said. They were wearing life jackets, but she wasn't taking any chances.

"You don't park a boat," Nathaniel corrected. "Weren't you listening to the captain? You dock a boat."

"Okay. Wait until the boat is docked before you get up."

The kids squirmed in their seats, then hopped up the minute the boat stopped moving. Although it was a nice day, there weren't many other people on the ferry, so Roz, Paul and the kids were on solid ground in a couple of minutes. The ferry was scheduled to leave in three hours, giving them plenty of time to explore but not enough time to get bored.

The island was beautiful. There was a long sandy beach to their left and grass and trees to their right. Naturally, the kids gravitated to the water and began gathering shells. She followed them, Paul by her side.

She watched the kids pick up sand dollars, Paul's words from earlier circling her mind. He'd promised—or had he threatened?—that they would continue their conversation. And just what would he say? More important, what was she going to say? She was still blown away to hear that he'd checked on her at night. He'd been so distant to her, so infernally polite, that she couldn't believe he'd actually do something like that.

Maybe she shouldn't be surprised. Paul had always taken his responsibilities seriously. From schoolwork to sports, he'd given 100 percent. He'd never slacked off at anything. Except their relationship. He'd put that on the back burner while he'd pursued his college education, giving her less and less attention as time went on. Looking back, she realized that she'd needed more from him than he'd had the ability to give. She'd needed the security that came from being loved and having someone she could count on, something it had been unfair to ask of him. He'd only been a kid. He'd needed to focus completely on his classes, but at the time, she'd felt abandoned. Lost.

Not that it mattered. The past was over. What troubled her now was knowing that Paul had witnessed her weakest moments. He'd had a front row seat to her emotional collapse and knew she'd been faking a strength she didn't possess. Yet he hadn't offered her any comfort. Instead, he'd observed her pain and then turned his back and walked away. And after knowing how scared she was, he'd continued to hold her at a distance.

If she needed further evidence that his concern had limits, she had it. So she couldn't allow herself to think his feelings toward her had softened just because he smiled at her and held her hand. He was simply doing what was necessary to help Suzanne through a hard patch. Roz needed to remember that.

"We'll never convince Suzanne everything between us is fine if you keep avoiding me."

Roz looked up and into Paul's serious eyes. She hadn't heard him approach and his nearness made her heart pound. Inhaling, she got a whiff of clean male combined with the salty air. Expelling a breath, she took a step back. She intended to protect her heart, but when he was this close, she had a hard time remembering the danger he presented.

"That's exactly what I'm talking about. Whenever I come near you, you back away." He stepped so close that they were practically touching to emphasize his point.

She backed away again, holding her hands in front of her as if that would freeze him in place. "Coming here was a mistake. In fact, this whole crazy idea is a mistake. Too much has happened for us to suddenly act like you don't hate me. You might be a good enough actor to pull it off, but I'm not. Maybe you should just go back to Florida and let me muddle along on my own. I'm getting better. Eventually, Suzanne will return to her usual self."

He frowned. "You've said so many things, I don't

know what to address first. There's not enough time and this isn't the place to get into a long discussion, so I'll sum up my answer in two words—no way."

"What?"

"You heard me." He looked over her shoulder and his frown turned into a smile.

She turned around and noticed they'd drawn the kids' attention. But while Nathaniel and Megan merely looked curious, Suzanne appeared nervous. She was sucking her thumb and her eyes were wide with worry. Her little body was as stiff as a board.

Paul leaned in closer and whispered furiously in her ear. "You still want to argue, or do you want to stick to the plan we agreed on? It's up to you." He held out his hand as if daring her to take it.

"Fine. You win." She grabbed his hand and squeezed it as hard as she could. She knew with her lack of strength she couldn't hurt him. Even at full strength, she'd only cause him mild discomfort. Still, he could at least pretend. But the frustrating man just laughed.

Roz refused to look at him and, instead, focused on her youngest daughter. Suzanne's body had lost some of its stiffness, and although she had pulled her thumb from her mouth, she wasn't quite smiling. Roz blew out a breath and then smiled at her little girl. "Uncle Paul told me that you've found a couple of sand dollars."

Suzanne nodded and opened her hand. "See?"

"Nice."

Nathaniel trotted over. "When are we going to see the horses?"

Roz glanced over at Paul, who shrugged. "I guess now, if you're finished here."

Megan scrambled to her feet and grabbed Roz's hand. "I'm ready."

"We don't have to ride them, do we?" Suzanne asked in a tiny voice.

"No," Roz replied. "These are wild horses. Nobody gets to ride them."

"That's too bad," Megan said. "I had fun that time I rode a horse on Mr. Jones's ranch. He rode with me."

"I rode by myself," Nathaniel bragged. That day at the Double J Ranch had been the highlight of Nathaniel's year. He hadn't stopped talking about it yet.

"I was scared," Suzanne admitted. "The horse was too big."

Laughing, Paul swooped down, grabbed Suzanne around her waist and settled her on his broad shoulders. "How about a horsy ride on Uncle Paul. I'm not big and scary."

Roz looked at him. With his well-defined chest, impressive biceps and sculpted abs, his appearance wasn't the least bit scary, but her body's reaction to him frightened her down to her toes. No matter how hard she tried to fight it, she found herself attracted to him. She consoled herself with the fact that most women would find him sexy. As long as she didn't act on that attraction, she would be okay.

Suzanne giggled and grabbed his head to hold on. Her laughter steadied the place in Roz's heart that still trembled with fear for her child.

"Look at me, Mommy," Suzanne called as Paul galloped over the land, his long legs eating the ground easily.

"I see. It looks like fun," Roz called, following at a more sedate pace.

"It is. Maybe Uncle Paul will give you a ride, too."

Roz's eyes flew to Paul's face. His smile was too wicked for a man who was interested in another woman. But then they were putting on a show for Suzanne. No emotions were involved. "I'm too heavy for that. But you go ahead and enjoy the ride."

"I don't know about you being too heavy. You probably don't weigh much more than Suzanne."

Suddenly self-conscious and painfully aware of the amount of weight she'd lost with her illness, Roz looked away. Her normal clothes no longer fit, hanging on her as if she were a little girl playing dress-up in her mother's clothes. She'd confided in Charlotte how depressed she felt every time she saw her reflection in a mirror. The next day, her friend had shown up with two shopping bags filled with new clothes. They were smaller than Roz's regular size, but she felt so much better dressed in clothes that fit. Being the good friend that she was, Charlotte had refused payment, telling Roz that every time she wore her new clothes she should remember that someone cared.

They followed the trail past tide pools and through the marsh until they reached a small hill. Nathaniel and Megan decided to race to the top.

“Wait. I want to race, too,” Suzanne said, wiggling on Paul’s shoulders. “Put me down, Uncle Paul.”

Paul stooped down, lifted Suzanne from his shoulders and then set her on the ground. She was off in a flash, her chubby legs pumping as she scrambled to catch up with her older siblings. Standing, Paul approached Roz, his face filled with remorse. “I didn’t mean to hurt your feelings, Roz.”

She shrugged, trying for nonchalance and failing miserably. She didn’t make the effort to smile. He’d see through it anyway.

He shoved his hands into the pockets of his jeans. “In a perfect world I would have said what I meant. Or at least I’d be able to go back in time and say what I meant.”

“Not too many perfect worlds around.”

“I know. So I’ll just explain. I was trying to say that you aren’t too heavy for me to carry. I’ve done it before, remember?”

Despite the fact that twelve years had passed since they’d been in love, she remembered every minute she’d spent wrapped in his arms. That was the problem. Like indelible ink, the past refused to be erased. It could be covered over for a while, but eventually it would work its way to the surface and become visible again.

"No. I'm the one who needs to apologize. I'm a little bit self-conscious about my appearance. I look in the mirror and a scarecrow stares back."

"You're being a bit harsh, don't you think?"

"Not hardly. All things considered, my looks shouldn't matter, but they do. I know I wasn't a beauty queen before, but I wasn't scrawny either." Paul started to speak and she raised her hand, cutting him off. "I wonder if part of the reason Suzanne worries about me dying is the fact that I look so terrible."

Paul closed the distance between them. Reaching out, he caressed her face. "That's not true. You're still a very beautiful woman. A desirable woman. Losing a few pounds and your hair hasn't changed that."

Roz leaned her face into his hand, letting herself bask in the feel of his skin, the warmth in his eyes. She missed human contact. It had been so long since a man other than a medical professional had touched her.

He placed his other hand on her cheek, cupping her face. The look in his eyes was so intense that her heart skipped a beat. "Don't worry, Roz. Everything will be fine. I promise."

"You can't know that." She was whispering, the intimacy of the moment taking her voice away. Was he really caressing her cheeks? And was she really allowing him to do so?

"I can. And I do." He leaned his forehead against hers as if putting his positive thoughts into her brain.

"Okay." She could believe almost anything when she was this close to him, including that he sincerely cared about her. It wasn't true, of course, but right now it didn't matter.

Paul pulled the seat belt over a drowsy Megan and clicked it closed while Roz fastened a sleeping Suzanne into her booster seat. Nathaniel was still awake, but he was much quieter than he'd been this morning. The excursion had exhausted the kids. Once they'd spotted the horses, they'd watched in awe as the powerful, beautiful animals enjoyed the freedom that nature granted them. When the kids grew bored, they'd raced up the hill and rolled down over and over again.

Paul had been concerned that the day would be too much for Roz. He'd tried to slow her down but didn't succeed as often as he would have liked. She hadn't wanted to hinder her kids, who were enjoying themselves. Nathaniel and the girls had wanted to see every sight and Roz had been pulled along. She hadn't complained once. As usual, she put her kids' happiness before everything else. But she needed to take care of herself, too. She was the glue that held the little family together. If anything happened to her, it would fall apart.

He waited until she'd fastened her seat belt before pulling out of the parking lot and heading home. After their time on the island, they'd taken the ferry back to the mainland and had a leisurely meal at a casual restaurant. Then they strolled through the quaint town, doing a bit of window-shopping. Roz spotted a shop that sold cuckoo clocks and they'd gone inside. She'd picked up several of the hand-carved clocks, studying every detail. When the kids grew restless, he'd offered to take them outside, but she'd turned him down. She'd taken one last look around, her eyes lingering on a clock she'd returned to over and over, and then they'd left.

The part of him that hadn't learned his lesson about how fickle Roz's heart could be had been tempted to go back and buy the clock for her. He hadn't. His brain had held him back. Such an act would be too revealing. He couldn't let her know that his resistance was crumbling, that he wasn't faking his concern.

Despite fighting it, his concern for her had begun growing a while ago. That's why he'd bought her new clothes. He'd heard her crying many nights. His heart had broken a little more each time and he'd grown frustrated by his inability to make things better.

Then he'd overheard her despairing over her wardrobe with her friend Charlotte. He might not be able to heal Roz, but he could help her feel better about her appearance. Roz would never have taken a gift from him, but she would accept one from her best friend. So he'd approached Charlotte and convinced her to buy Roz clothes that fit. Money hadn't been an object. The smile on Roz's face and her improved confidence was worth any price.

He glanced over at her. She'd leaned back against the headrest and closed her eyes. Her lips parted as she blew out a soft sigh.

He took a moment to study her. Yes her face was thinner, but it was still stunning. Her cheekbones were high and her eyes a beautiful shade of brown. But it was her lips that drew him like a magnet drew steel. They were full and made to be kissed. By him.

Shaking his head, he chased that thought away and switched the radio to a classical station he knew Roz enjoyed. He was just thankful that Roz couldn't read his mind.

Chapter Eight

The ground beneath Roz was moving, shifting back and forth. The motion was steady, like a boat cutting through the waves. She lifted her face, but instead of being spritzed by water, she encountered warmth. Inhaling deeply, she got a whiff of clean male with a hint of the outdoors. Something wasn't right. She wasn't on the ferry. The ride had ended hours ago and she and Paul had loaded the kids into the car for the long drive home.

Maybe she was still in the car. No. The motion wasn't quite right. This didn't feel like the smooth ride of Paul's SUV. No matter. It was comfortable so she wasn't inclined to figure it out.

She heard giggling and knew she had to open her eyes. Just then, she felt herself falling, and heart pounding, she reached for something to hold on to. Her eyes sprang open and she looked around. She was in Paul's arms, holding on to him for dear life. He lowered her onto the sofa while the kids looked on, their eyes not missing a thing.

"You fell asleep," Megan said.

Roz rubbed her eyes and covered a yawn. "I guess I did."

"I was scared you might not wake up," Suzanne whispered, her thumb hovering near her mouth. She leaned against Roz's leg as if in need of contact.

"Why?" Roz decided that the best comfort she could give her daughter was to point out how normal it was to fall asleep in the car. Grinning, she gently poked each of her daughters in the stomach. "I'm not the only one who was sleeping. You girls were asleep before I was."

"I'm the only one who stayed awake," Nathaniel said, puffing out his chest.

"Hey, don't forget about me. I was awake, too," Paul added.

"You had to stay awake, Uncle Paul. You were driving," Megan pointed out.

"True. Now, who's hungry? I could go for some soup and a grilled cheese sandwich."

"And potato chips?" Suzanne gave a little smile as she walked toward Paul.

He lifted her into his arms. "Sure. Why not?"

"I'll help," Roz said, starting to stand.

"That's not necessary. It won't take more than a minute. Besides, too many cooks will spoil the meal."

Roz leaned back, stretching her legs in front of her. "You'll get no argument from me. I'll just keep relaxing."

She watched as Paul strode into the kitchen, Suzanne still in his arms. The sound of pots rattling was soon followed by the aroma of bread frying. Fifteen minutes later, they all were seated in the living room, television trays in front of them as they ate. One of the kids' favorite shows blared from the TV.

"I like eating in here," Megan said, slurping her tomato soup. A little dribbled onto her chin and she wiped it off with the back of her hand. "We should do this every day."

"Yeah," Nathaniel agreed. "That way we can watch TV."

"Every once in a while is okay," Roz said, "but I would miss talking about our days. I wouldn't know about your apples and onions. Then I wouldn't be able to find out what made you happy and what made you sad."

"I didn't have any onions today," Megan answered, and the other kids quickly agreed that nothing had made them unhappy.

"That's wonderful. What about apples?"

"The horses are my apple," Megan said. "I liked watching them run around. Especially when they were in the water."

"That was great. But I liked riding the boat best," Nathaniel added. "That's my apple."

"What was your apple?" Paul asked Suzanne.

"I liked when you were carrying Mommy."

"That was my favorite part, too," Paul said, then looked over at Roz.

Suddenly the center of attention, Roz felt her cheeks grow warm. She tried to look away from Paul's probing eyes but couldn't. It was as if he was trying to read her mind to discover her hidden secrets. Or worse, maybe he wanted to peer into her heart and search out her private feelings. She couldn't let him know that after all this time, after all these years, she was falling for him again. That would make things between them even more uncomfortable. Not to mention the beating her pride would take when he told her he didn't return her feelings, as he no doubt would. Some days pride was the only thing she had.

"My apple was seeing all the different kinds of birds, especially the babies. I liked the way they looked around, trying to see their world."

"Me, too," Megan added. "The baby birds were so cute."

"Didn't you like it when Uncle Paul carried you?"

Suzanne pressed, clearly displeased that Roz's answer wasn't the one she'd wanted to hear.

More than you could ever imagine.

"Sure," Roz said, trying to sound casual even as her heart was jumping up and down in excitement at the memory. "But remember, I was asleep for most of it." But when she had awakened, she'd felt pure bliss from her head to her toes. For a moment, all had been right in the world. Of course, that was just a fantasy. Nothing had changed between them or in her life.

"We should go back there again," Megan said.

Roz flashed her oldest daughter a grin, more than happy to change the subject. "Definitely. But there are so many other fun places to go."

"There's going to be a carnival in a few weeks," Nathaniel pointed out. "Bobby's going with his dad and Charlotte. We should go, too."

"That's a good idea," Roz replied. It was already on the list of fun activities that she and Paul were considering. It depended on her energy that day. They'd chosen a children's puppet show for the next activity. Thankfully, that would require much less energy. She was loath to admit it, but she still tired easily.

The conversation moved to other topics and she listened absently as the others chatted among themselves. They laughed often and even little Suzanne giggled a few times.

Paul insisted on cleaning the kitchen and helping

Megan and Suzanne with their baths. When the girls were dressed in their favorite pajamas, Roz joined them in their bedroom for prayers and a bedtime story. It was Suzanne's turn to choose the book. The girls enjoyed fairy tales, but it was a little surprising when Suzanne chose "The Three Pigs." Not that Roz was complaining. She didn't want her daughters to grow up believing some prince was going to rescue them from the troubles they were certain to encounter in life. Not to mention that Roz was sick to death of reading a sappy, romantic story that ended happily ever after when her life was such a mess.

And wasn't this whole line of thought just ridiculous? She looked up and realized that she was sitting frozen on Megan's bed, the open book in her hands.

"I'll read tonight if you want," Paul offered.

"Thanks, but no. Reading to my girls is the favorite part of my day." She snuggled the girls sitting on either side of her a bit closer. On those occasions when she'd been too sick to read, Paul had taken over story time. Even though she'd been having good days, Paul remained part of the ritual, sitting on the foot of the bed.

Roz read the words, telling the familiar story of the pigs. She looked up to find Paul staring at her, an unfathomable look in his eyes. Disconcerted, she looked back at the page and read the first words she saw.

"You said that already, Mommy," Megan complained.

"Sorry. I guess I lost my place." She quickly resumed reading, hoping she was in the right spot. No one grumbled, so she guessed she'd gotten it right. Now if only her voice would stop quivering.

Finally, she reached the end, with the big bad wolf huffing and puffing but failing to blow the house in. The girls cheered and Suzanne hopped off Megan's bed and jumped into her own. Roz tucked them in and kissed them on the forehead. Suzanne wrapped her arms around Roz's neck and held on for a long moment before releasing her and snuggling under her blanket. Both little girls were sound asleep before Roz and Paul were out of the room.

They crossed the hall to Nathaniel's room, said good-night to him, then stepped back into the hallway where they faced each other. Roz didn't know whether Paul intended to go to his room or go back downstairs. Standing this close to him in the dimly lit hallway left her tongue-tied and unable to ask.

He seemed equally incapable of speaking, so they continued to stare at each other. After a long moment, he blew out a breath. "How are you feeling?"

She was so tired of answering that question and barely kept from snapping. There was more to her than nausea, vomiting and diarrhea. She was still a woman. "I'm fine."

"Good." He nodded. "Then we can continue our conversation from earlier."

Suddenly her knees wobbled. She knew from experience that Paul could be stubborn when he thought the situation warranted it. If he wanted to talk about feelings—or whatever—they were going to talk. If not now, then later. She didn't want this conversation hanging over her head.

"Okay. How about a mug of cocoa?" she offered.

"For you. I'd rather have a cup of coffee."

She grinned. "You never were a fan of chocolate."

He smiled in return and her heart skipped a beat. "And you never liked coffee."

"The great aroma is false advertising. It doesn't taste a thing like it smells."

They walked to the kitchen together then set about making their beverages. She heated the milk slowly, then added squares of Hershey's chocolate, stirring until the chocolate melted. She poured the liquid into her favorite mug, added a dollop of whipped cream, stretching out the process as long as she could, then sat at the table.

"Do you think you'll be more comfortable on the sofa?" Paul asked, standing in the doorway that led to the front room.

Physically, definitely. The soft cushions were preferable to the hard wooden chairs. Emotionally, no way. She needed the barrier the table provided. If she got too comfortable, she might let down her guard and reveal things better left hidden. Like how she'd do just about anything to have a second chance with him. "This is good."

Nodding, he pulled out the chair across from her. He stirred cream and sugar into his coffee before looking up at her. Blowing out a breath, he leaned back in his chair and crossed his arms across his muscular chest. "So you think I hate you."

She rocked back. Talk about cutting to the chase. Well she could be direct, too. "Hate might be a little strong, but you don't like me. I've known that for years. You're always polite as can be, but there's no warmth in your voice. And your eyes could give a polar bear frostbite. And before you tell me that I'm imagining things, look at the situation we're in. What if Suzanne has sensed your feelings and the tension between us and it's adding to her stress about my disease?"

"Maybe I've been cold at times. Unnecessarily so, to be honest. But that doesn't mean I hate you. I don't." He rubbed a hand over his close-cropped hair. It was still jet-black without a hint of gray. "Truth be told, I'm not sure how I feel about you. I'm conflicted, you know?"

She nodded. She understood since she was confused herself. On one hand, she was grateful to him for coming when she'd asked. On the other hand, she resented his presence and hated needing him. On another hand, she was becoming more attracted to him every day and wanted another chance to see if they could get it right this time. But on another hand…well, a person only had two hands. Forgetting that was further proof that she was a walking mess of contradictions.

"But I love those kids," he continued. "I'm certain about that. And I will do anything to make sure that they're okay."

"About that. I know you care about them, but I don't want you lying to them. That's not right."

"When have I lied?"

"You told Nathaniel you'd take him out on your boat."

He nodded.

"You and I both know that isn't going to happen. But he doesn't. When he discovers that you didn't mean it, he'll be heartbroken."

Paul's eyes narrowed. "Who said I didn't mean it?"

"Come on, Paul. You've never taken him on your boat before. You're here now but you'll get back to your life in Florida, leaving us behind. I know that, but Nathaniel doesn't. He loves you and believes what you say. He's going to be devastated when you don't keep this promise."

Paul was as still as stone, yet he seemed to vibrate with anger. But she wouldn't take back her words. Her child's happiness was at stake. If she didn't stand up for Nathaniel, who would? She knew what it felt like to be left behind and forgotten.

Reaching out, she touched his hand. "I know you don't mean to set him up for disappointment. But that's not going to make it hurt any less."

"I never say things I don't mean."

She could have reminded him that he'd promised to come back for her but had forgotten about her easily enough. Instead, she said nothing. Her hurt feelings years ago weren't the issue.

"I told Nathaniel I would take him on my boat and I intend to do just that."

"How? Your boat is in Florida. We're here. Are you going to take him home with you? When? How? He has school and you have work. A life to get back to."

He glared at her but didn't answer.

"I take it you didn't think about any of that. You didn't need to. You can simply make promises. But I have to think about these things. I'm Nathaniel's mother."

"And I'm his uncle. That might not matter to you, but it matters to me."

"I didn't say it didn't matter," Roz protested. The conversation was veering off in a direction she hadn't anticipated. "I'm just asking you to be careful not to make promises to my kids. You might not mean to hurt them, but trust me when I say that it won't take away the pain."

Paul blew out a breath. She thought he might press his point further, but he just looked grim instead. "Fine."

They sat in uncomfortable silence for a few more minutes. Roz looked into her mug of chocolate, the desire to drink it gone. It was lukewarm now anyway. Standing, she dumped the remaining liquid into the sink. "Are we finished here? I really need to get some sleep."

Paul looked at her for a long minute. He nodded. "Yeah. We're finished."

She knew that he was talking about more than that conversation. He was talking about them. The possibility of giving a romantic relationship another try. Her heart ached at the realization that there wouldn't be a second chance for them, but she knew he was right. They were finished. They had been for a long time.

Chapter Nine

Roz closed the small suitcase and then took a deep breath. She'd been dreading this moment for days. Weeks. She'd finished her last round of chemotherapy and now that the chemo was no longer in her system, the surgeon was ready to operate. The chemo had shrunk the tumor, making its removal easier and safer.

But first, she had to say goodbye to her children. She'd been preparing them for a couple of days, and they knew she would be in the hospital in Charlotte for a few days after surgery. Her intention had been to get them used to the idea, but it hadn't had the desired effect. Suzanne had become clingier and had refused to sleep in her own bed, insisting on sleeping with Roz. Neither girl would go to the youth center after school or on weekends, choosing to stay at home with Roz. Nathaniel had become more protective of his sisters, repeatedly assuring Roz that he would take care of them.

"Ready?" Paul asked, coming into her room. He took the bag from her and his eyes searched hers.

"I'm scared," she admitted. Her voice wobbled.

"I know. But everything is going to be fine," he said. That had become his mantra of the past week. She didn't know if he was reassuring her or himself.

He released the bag and put his arm around her waist, pulling her into a gentle hug. He rubbed his hands up and down her back in soothing circles. Although she knew it was dangerous to her heart to rely on him too much, she leaned into his embrace, drawing comfort from his nearness. After a few moments, they drew apart, though he stayed near as they walked to the front room.

"It's time for me to leave," Roz announced. She tried to sound cheerful, but her joy sounded phony even to her own ears. She looked at her kids, huddled against each other on the sofa, and her prepared speech fled. They looked so small sitting there. So vulnerable.

"Okay, Mom," Nathaniel said, tightening his arms around his sisters, who sat on either side of him.

"I'll be home soon."

"After your operation?" Megan asked.

"Yes." Roz had explained that she was having surgery to remove the sick parts of her body. Fortunately she didn't need a hysterectomy.

"Then you'll be well?" Megan asked. She'd asked this question repeatedly over the past couple of days.

"Then I'll be well. It might take me a little while to get strong again."

"And your hair will grow back so you won't be ball-headed anymore," Suzanne said. She didn't like seeing Roz's bald head, so Roz made a point of wearing a scarf.

Roz cringed and fought the urge to touch it. "Yes. But that'll take time, too."

"I'll take care of everything," Nathaniel promised.

"I know you will," Roz said. "Now, everyone give me a hug."

The kids jumped to their feet and she gave them each a hug. Then, as if by unspoken agreement, they swarmed her as one, holding on for dear life. She squeezed them tight, not wanting to let them go.

"We need to get going," Paul said, detangling the kids from her and leading her out the door. The kids followed and stood close together on the porch. Charlotte, who was staying with them until Paul returned, stood behind them. Roz got in the car and looked at them through the passenger window as Paul drove away. She didn't face forward until the house disappeared from sight.

“They’ll be fine,” Paul promised.

“I know.” Her voice revealed the doubt and sorrow she felt. But what else could she say?

“You won’t be gone that long.”

“It’ll feel like forever.”

“I know. But it won’t be.”

“If something happens to me...”

“It won’t.” He turned on the radio, putting an end to the conversation he clearly didn’t want to have. She didn’t press him because she didn’t want to have that talk either. She didn’t even want to consider the possibility of the worst occurring. But there was a heaviness in the air and in her spirit that prevented her from talking or thinking about anything else. Paul seemed to have the same problem, because he didn’t say another word on the entire drive to the hospital.

When they arrived, he parked and they walked side by side to the entrance. She’d practically memorized the written instructions and maps she’d been provided, so she led him to the registration area.

A middle-aged woman was sitting at the check-in desk, and, within minutes, Roz had been admitted. A nurse greeted them and led Roz to her room.

“I guess you need to leave?” Roz asked Paul. She couldn’t imagine he’d want to stay. Though things between them weren’t as tense as they’d been when he’d arrived, they still had a hard time communicating. Nothing ever came out the way she wanted it to.

It was as if her thoughts took a twisting road from her brain to her mouth.

He looked surprised and then shook his head. "No. Charlotte will stay with the kids until I get back."

Relief surged through her. "Thanks."

He closed his hand over hers. "I told you before that you're not alone. I'm here for the long haul, so just relax."

Warmth filled her heart and she smiled. For the first time in a long time she felt at peace. Maybe she'd been wrong. Perhaps Paul actually did care for her. Maybe instead of just assuming the worst about his motives, she should give him the benefit of the doubt.

The nurse brought in a gown and directed Roz to change into it.

"I'll step outside," Paul said. He gave her hand a gentle squeeze before he left.

This was really happening. A bunch of emotions bombarded her as she took off her clothes, put on the hospital gown and then got into the bed. A minute later, the door opened a few inches and Paul's face appeared.

"You decent?"

"Yes."

He stepped all the way into the room and sat at the chair beside her bed. She had a single room, so she was guaranteed to have privacy for any conversations they had. "I called Charlotte. She said the kids are fine."

"Thanks. I don't know what I would do without her."

"Do you need anything?" Paul asked.

"Just for this all to be over."

"If I had the power to make it so, it would be."

Paul's heartfelt words felt so good, Roz basked in them. Even after he gave her an awkward kiss on the cheek that made her toes tingle and promised to see her after surgery, she mulled them over and over, happiness floating through her. She might be able to get through this after all.

Paul clenched his jaw and paced to the other end of the hallway, not stopping until his nose was mere inches away from the pale blue wall. The hospital administrators had probably chosen this paint color because they thought it soothing. It wasn't.

He inhaled deeply, then slowly blew out a ragged breath and tried to assure himself that Roz would be fine. But after enduring months of chemotherapy that had left her weak and violently ill, he was worried. Paul knew this operation was the next step in a solid treatment plan, but that didn't lessen his concern. He might not be in love with her, but he'd come to care a great deal for her. Probably more than was wise.

"Mr. Stephens?"

Paul jerked and turned to face the nurse. She was

smiling, which he took as a good sign. Or as close to good as one could expect under the circumstances.

"How is Roz?"

"She's out of surgery and on her way to recovery. Dr. Perry will be out to speak with you soon, so you should return to the waiting room."

He looked around. He'd managed to walk from the waiting area into the serenity room without being aware of it. But being here didn't do anything to alleviate his worry. Nothing short of seeing Roz with his own eyes would do that.

Paul followed the nurse through a glass door and down an antiseptic-smelling corridor to the waiting area. He contemplated taking a chair before deciding he had too much nervous energy to sit still and didn't relish the thought of bouncing up and down in front of an audience.

"Martin family."

Paul crossed the room in two long strides. "That's me. How is Roz?"

The surgeon pulled a cap off his head, revealing curly salt-and-pepper hair. "The surgery went well. I'm confident that we got all of the cancer."

"What is her prognosis? Is she healed?"

The doctor sighed and wiped a hand down his face. "It's difficult to answer that. People with cervical cancer are living longer than they were only five years ago. But I never use the word healed." The surgeon blew out another breath and seemed to weigh his next words carefully, clearly unaware that with each passing second Paul was inching closer to the edge of insanity. “That said, I’m cautiously optimistic in this case. Ms. Martin is young and in otherwise good health.”

Paul frowned. That was no help. He needed something definite. Something conclusive. He needed the doctor to say that Roz was cured and the cancer would never come back. He needed the doctor to promise that Roz would live a long life.

“That’s the best answer I can give you. Trust me, this is good news.” The doctor clapped his hand on Paul’s shoulder and gave what Paul supposed was meant to be a reassuring squeeze before walking away.

Paul exhaled in an effort to blow away his tension. Though Roz was probably groggy, she might be able to sense his feelings. It wouldn’t be good for her to know he was worried.

Several minutes dragged by before the nurse returned and led him to the recovery room. He glanced inside and his heart dropped. Roz looked so frail. She’d always been petite, but now she was positively fragile. And she was sound asleep.

“It’ll probably be an hour or so before the anesthesia wears off. If you want to get something to eat, we can call you when she wakes up.”

Paul nodded. Instead of going to the cafeteria, he returned to the waiting room. He called Charlotte to let her know the surgery went well, then spoke with each of the kids.

An hour and a half later, he was informed that Roz had awakened and he was escorted back to her bedside. Her eyelids fluttered, then opened. She stared at him and lifted a hand a few inches before dropping it back onto the bed. “Hi.”

He sat by her side and took her hand into his, careful not to squeeze it. Despite his worry, he felt a charge at the contact. He pushed the reaction aside. Hadn't he made up his mind that she was wrong for him? Not only that, she was recovering from major surgery. “How are you feeling?”

“Tired.” Her voice was so soft he had to lean in to hear. “And a little achy.”

Roz had never been one to complain, so for all he knew, she could be in excruciating pain.

“Rest.” He released her hand, placing it beneath the thin blanket covering her. “Sleep is what you need now.”

“Have you talked to the kids?”

“Yes. They're fine.”

“Okay.” She sighed then closed her eyes. A minute later, she was breathing steadily. Paul sat in the chair beside the bed and watched as she slept, counting her breaths as if to reassure himself that she was still alive. Finally satisfied that all was well, he rose and left, refusing to allow himself one last look at her. His concern was morphing into something more.

Something like love. Something he needed to fight before it overwhelmed his common sense and took over his life.

"I really can walk," Roz said to the young patient transporter. It seemed as if she'd spent the past few months lying down or sitting in her recliner, too weak to move while others cared for her kids. Now she looked forward to doing things for herself, such as walk out of this hospital.

Her operation had gone well, and, fortunately, she hadn't had any complications during her recovery. The day of the surgery had provided several shocks to her system. She'd walked into the hospital that morning but had been unable to scoot from the gurney to her bed mere hours later. Sitting up had been painful and she'd been weak and found walking exhausting. Still, she'd pressed on and now, four days after her arrival, she was able to return home to her family.

"I know you can. But the wheelchair is protocol. Besides, it's much faster. You'll be with your family sooner if you take the ride."

"Those are the magic words," Roz said, settling into the seat and putting her bag on her lap. She hadn't seen her kids in what felt like forever and her arms ached to hold them. Ever since she'd been diagnosed with cancer, she'd harbored a fear that she wouldn't get to seen them grow up. That they would be orphaned as she'd been. Now that she'd survived chemo and surgery, that worry had diminished. She knew she had a long road to travel, but she was starting to see the light at the end of the tunnel.

Paul was waiting for her at the hospital entrance. He'd been by her side earlier as the nurse explained the post-op instructions. He'd even asked a few questions, then had gone to get the car so she wouldn't have to walk through the parking lot.

Spotting her, Paul quickly emerged from the SUV. Ever courteous, he helped her from the wheelchair and into the passenger seat. They reached for her seat belt at the same time and their hands brushed. Electricity shot through her, and her breath caught in her throat. Paul had visited her throughout her hospital stay. His presence had been comforting. More comforting than she would ever admit. She'd looked forward to seeing him. Each day, their conversations had come more easily and they'd laughed together often. After years of animosity, they were finally becoming friends.

After fastening her seat belt, she blew out a breath, hoping to rid herself of this crazy attraction. At the rate it was growing, she'd be head over heels before long.

"How do you feel?" Paul asked.

"I don't foresee a marathon in my future, but I feel better than I'd expected."

"That's good to hear."

He smiled and her heart lurched. Now more than ever, she needed to get a handle on her attraction. Paul wasn't interested in giving them a second chance. Not only that, he would be leaving soon. If she fell in love with him again, it wouldn't end well for her. This time, if her heart got broken, she'd have no one to blame but herself.

Roz tuned the radio to a station playing smooth jazz and closed her eyes, letting the sounds float over her body. She didn't intend to fall asleep, but there was no harm in relaxing.

The car lurched and Roz jerked awake. She pried her eyes open and looked around. Trees swayed in the breeze and baskets overflowing with orange and gold fall flowers lined the sidewalk. They were on Main Street in Sweet Briar. She'd slept most of the two-hour drive from Charlotte.

"Ah, good, you're awake. The kids might worry if they saw you sleeping so deeply." Roz nodded. She'd overheard Suzanne ask if her mommy slept so much because she was going to die. Paul had done his best to reassure her, but Roz knew her daughter still worried. Suzanne often shook Roz awake when she'd slept too long for the little girl's comfort.

"Of course, I could tell them that you've always fallen asleep in the car," Paul continued with a mischievous grin, "but they probably wouldn't believe me."

"Only when I'm not driving," she corrected with

a grin of her own. "The soothing motion of a moving car just knocks me out."

"And makes you drool."

"Drool?" She swiped her hand across her mouth.

He laughed and her insides quivered. He stopped at a stop sign and grinned again. "And snore. Loudly."

"Now I know you're lying. I have never snored in my life."

"Trust me, you were calling the hogs a few minutes ago." He glanced in the rearview mirror. "Just checking to be sure none are following us."

"Ha ha." She poked him in the shoulder. It had been years since they'd had this much fun together. She was almost sorry for the ride to come to an end.

Paul pulled onto the street and parked in front of Roz's house. A huge banner reading Welcome Home Mommy hung across the front porch. The letters were lopsided and each word was a different size. Colorful flowers dotted with glitter created a border around the edge of the banner. Rainbow ribbons tied around the porch rails fluttered in the breeze. Her heart filled with unspeakable joy. She turned to Paul, who was looking at her. "Did you know about this?"

He patted her hand. "Of course. They missed you. Working on this helped keep them occupied. Sit still. I'll help you out."

The front door opened and her children raced down the stairs and to the SUV. Charlotte followed at a more sedate pace. Roz didn't know how she'd ever repay her friend for all she'd done for her and her family.

Paul nudged the kids back so he could open her door. Riding in Paul's top-of-the-line Mercedes was heavenly, but she was starting to ache from the long ride. She brushed the discomfort aside, thrilled to see her family again.

The kids stood like statues, staring at her. What was wrong?

"Uncle Paul and Charlotte said we have to be careful not to hurt you," Nathaniel explained. "Will it hurt if we hug you?"

Roz shook her head and held out her arms. If there was pain, it would be more than worth it. She couldn't bear not holding her children for one more second.

"Carefully," Paul stated firmly, blocking them with his arm as if expecting them to stampede. "One at a time."

Nathaniel was closest, so she pulled her son into a strong embrace and kissed his cheek. Despite Paul's admonition, Megan charged next, trampling Roz's foot as she wrapped her chubby arms around her waist, squeezing for all she was worth. Roz must have made a sound, because Paul was immediately there, gently disengaging her daughter's arms.

"Let's let Suzanne say hello, too." He gestured to her youngest daughter, who stood a ways away. Though she had rushed down with the others, she stood frozen, staring at Roz. Then her lower lip began to tremble and she burst into tears. Roz's heart broke as she hurried to her youngest child, pulling her into her embrace. "It's all right. I'm here."

"I missed you, Mommy. You were gone a long time."

"I missed you, too. All of you." Roz included her other children in her gaze.

"I was scared you were never coming back."

"Oh, baby. I told you that I would."

Suzanne just nodded and leaned her head against Roz's side.

After a moment, Paul stepped up. "Let's get everyone inside."

"Okay," Charlotte said, taking Suzanne's hand and leading the way into the house. Megan and Nathaniel followed. "Come on, guys. Let's get your presents."

"Are you okay?" Paul asked, wrapping his arms around her in a gentle embrace.

She nodded, then pressed her face against the solid wall of his chest.

Being in his arms brought back memories she hadn't dared let out of their hidden place in her heart. They'd broken free, bombarding her as they raced through her mind, stirring up her emotions, and it took every effort she had to restrain them and box them up again. She lifted her head and her eyes collided with his. Dark brown and fringed with thick black lashes, his eyes were filled with compassion. She wished she saw love there as well but knew she never would. Their time had come and gone.

Gathering herself, she took a deep breath, then leaned on him as they walked into the house, where her children awaited her. Her past may be over, but her present was still good. And for the first time since her diagnosis, she had hope that the future would be even better.

Chapter Ten

Paul watched as Roz gushed over the gifts he'd helped the children make. He'd wanted to buy presents, but the kids didn't have much money between them. Although they received a weekly allowance for doing their chores, the girls were flat broke. He'd learned that they spent their money as soon as they got it, and not a minute later. He smiled as he recalled how Megan had turned her pants pockets inside out and Suzanne had shaken her empty piggy bank to emphasize the point. Nathaniel had most of his money, but he was saving it to buy a video game and was unwilling to part with it. Paul had offered to advance the money, but the kids rejected that idea right out of hand. If you pay for it, they'll be your gifts, Nathaniel had reasoned.

So they'd had to get creative. None of the kids had seen this as a problem. It's okay, Megan had insisted, Mommy likes it when we make her stuff. She says it's her favorite kind of present.

He knew that. The girls brought home masterpieces from the youth center on a regular basis and Roz had loved every one. But then Carmen Knight, the volunteer art teacher, was a famous artist. Naturally, they would create wonderful projects with her guidance. But she hadn't been at the youth center this week so the job of helping them fell to him.

Unfortunately, he wasn't the least bit artistic. As a businessman, he didn't need to be. Luckily, the kids had ideas of their own.

Nathaniel had thought of the banner. Paul had purchased the material, convincing the kids that he didn't have skills but wanted to contribute to the gift. Nathaniel had sketched the words in pencil and then all three kids had painted them. The girls added flowers, stickers and streamers. He'd tried to draw the line at glitter, but Suzanne's eyes had welled with tears and Megan had glared at him for making her sister cry. In the end, they'd used glitter.

He'd had the foresight to have them work in the backyard, so he didn't have to clean clumps of glue and glitter off furniture. Naturally, the girls had gotten glitter into their hair. Although he'd become adept at braids and twists, he knew better than to try to shampoo it out. He'd taken them to Fit To Be Dyed hair salon and let a professional handle the task. The girls loved the special treatment and he'd been awarded hero status.

"This is beautiful," Roz exclaimed, pulling his attention back to her. She was holding a framed picture of wildflowers Megan had found in a coloring book. Determined to stay within the lines, she'd taken nearly an hour to complete it. She'd scrawled her first and last names in a jumble of uppercase and lowercase letters across the back, using a different color crayon for each letter. She'd been disappointed when he told her that her name wouldn't be visible once the picture was matted and framed, but she'd been thrilled with the final result. Roz gave her oldest daughter a gentle squeeze and kissed the top of her head. "Thanks, sweetie."

"Open Suzanne's next," Megan urged.

Roz flashed her youngest child a smile and patted the place next to her. "I can't wait to see what it is."

Suzanne sat down and leaned her head against Roz's side. "It's not as pretty as Megan's."

"Sure it is," Megan said staunchly, ever the loyal big sister. "It's beautiful."

Smiling, Suzanne leaned her head against Roz's breast and hugged her around her neck. Roz winced and Paul practically felt her pain. It took everything he had not to unwrap Suzanne's arms and move her a safe distance away from Roz. He knew neither mother nor daughter would appreciate his interference. He did go and stand nearer to them. Roz lifted an eyebrow but otherwise didn't acknowledge his closer presence. She tore away the wrapping paper, then pulled out a framed picture. Suzanne hadn't been happy with the pictures in the coloring books, so she'd drawn her own. He hadn't been able to make heads or tails of the blurred ovals and triangles with lines sticking out the sides and bottom, but he'd known better than to say that. "I love it," Roz exclaimed.

"You do?" Suzanne asked, lifting her head and looking at Roz, her expression a combination of doubt and amazement.

"Absolutely. Tell me why you decided to draw this."

"Because I like Shadow, the dog from the ranch, and I wish we had a dog." She pointed to the little black blur in a sea of green that could be a dog if you looked at it from the right angle. "This is me and Megan playing with him." She then pointed to the biggest shape. "I didn't want to ride the horse, but I still thought it was pretty. This is Nathaniel riding the horse. He wasn't scared."

"I love this picture. Every time I look at it, I'll think about the happy day you had at the Double J Ranch. And that will make me happy. Thank you, baby."

Nathaniel approached, his gift in hand. "I didn't draw a picture."

"That's okay." Roz took the gift. She unwrapped it and then smiled at her son.

"It's a poem," Nathaniel said.

"I see."

"Read it, Mommy," Suzanne said, snuggling closer.

"Okay. It's entitled 'My Mom.'" Then she recited:

"You are the best mom in the world. That is true,
I don't know what we would do without you.
You love us even when we are bad,
You are the best mom anyone ever had.
You are pretty, nice and fun,
I would not trade you for anyone.
I love you, Mom, you know that's true,
There is no one as good as you."

Roz's voice trembled as she read the last words and Paul had to swallow the lump in his throat. Damn. His feelings were getting out of control. If he wasn't careful, he'd fall under her spell again. He knew he needed to keep her at a distance, but the more he was around her, the harder that became.

"It's wonderful," she said, then kissed Nathaniel's cheek. "All of my gifts are wonderful. Thank you all."

"You're welcome, Mommy," the girls chimed in unison.

Paul could tell that Roz was beginning to fade. Her smile seemed forced and she shifted in her seat as if in pain. It was time to step in. "Okay, guys, your mom is tired. She needs a nap."

"You can't make Mommy take a nap," Megan protested. "She's big. Big people don't take naps."

"Sometimes they do," he countered, lifting Suzanne from Roz's lap and setting her on her feet.

"Like when they might die?" Suzanne whispered, her eyes wide with fear. Roz's illness had been difficult on all of them, but Suzanne continued to have the hardest time coping. Paul tried, but he hadn't been able to convince her that Roz would be okay. Her hospital stay had set Suzanne back quite a bit.

"Mommy's not going to die." Megan punctuated her statement by stomping her foot.

Nathaniel wrapped an arm across his sisters' shoulders and drew them close, protecting them from a world that had become a scary place.

"Megan's right. I'm not going to die," Roz said. "I'm just tired. I'll take a nap and then make dinner. Okay?"

The kids nodded but they were still subdued. Paul helped Roz stand. She swayed a little and he held her more tightly, careful to be gentle. Her sweet scent surrounded him as if tempting him with images of a potential future together. Once, he'd dreamed of making a life with her. Heck, she'd been the entire dream. She'd destroyed more than his plans when she betrayed him. She'd ripped out his heart and then shredded it. It had taken him years to get over the hurt. No matter how soft her skin was or how comfortably she fit in his arms, he knew better than to get swept away by the moment. That would only lead to heartache.

"Can you make it on your own?" He suddenly needed more distance between them, but he wouldn't let her go if she'd only fall flat on her face. At least, that's what he told himself as he continued to hold her pressed against his side.

She blew out a breath before speaking. He felt her heart pounding against his chest, saw the pulse thumping in her throat. "I think so."

Slowly moving away from him, she took one staggering step and then another before gripping his wrist. Without thinking, he swept her into his arms. She gasped but otherwise made no complaint, her silence telling him all he needed to know.

"Why are you carrying Mommy?" Suzanne asked.

"I'm carrying her for the same reason I carry you to bed sometimes."

"Because she likes it?"

"Because she likes it," he confirmed. And though he was loath to admit it, he liked it, too. Roz was thinner than she'd been years ago, but she still fit in his arms like she'd been made for him. They fit together like puzzle pieces he'd been finding all over the house. That was a ridiculous thought. Life wasn't a child's game.

Paul circled the room, deftly avoiding a dollhouse and scattered crayons as he made his way to Roz's first-floor bedroom.

"I'll turn down the blankets," Megan cried, running ahead of him.

"Me, too," Suzanne added, chasing after her sister.

"I'm worried about Suzanne," Roz whispered. "I thought she was improving, but now I'm not so sure."

"Remember, we aren't supposed to expect a miracle," he said although he was worried, too. "Now that you're home, she'll bounce back."

"I hope you're right."

So did he. "I am."

"Look, it's all ready," Megan said as he stepped into the room.

"Thank you," Roz said. "You girls are wonderful."

Paul set her on the bed then got the peach gown he knew was her favorite.

She held out her hands. "I can get dressed on my own."

He nodded. "Come on, girls, let's give your mom some privacy."

Megan hopped across the floor on one foot, her new favorite way of getting from place to place, but Suzanne didn't budge. "Aren't you going to kiss

Mommy's cheek before she goes to sleep? You always kiss mine."

His eyes flew to Roz, who was looking at him, a thousand different emotions flitting across her face, none staying long enough for him to name. "Sure. I'll come back after your mom has changed."

Roz made a strangled sound. For a moment, he tried to figure out what her reaction meant, then decided it didn't matter.

Roz tried to slow her galloping heart. She needed to rein in her feelings before they raced ahead of her. So Paul was going to kiss her cheek. What was the big deal? It wasn't as if he wanted to kiss her. That would be a big deal. He was only going to brush his lips against her cheek because her daughter put him on the spot. The kiss wouldn't last longer than one second. Surely she could maintain an image of indifference for that long.

Pulling off her top, she tugged on her gown, stood briefly as she wiggled out of her skirt, then dropped back onto the mattress. Unbelievably, that little bit of activity had her panting like she'd run three miles, something she hadn't done in longer than she cared to remember. Running was one of the many things she was looking forward to doing once she was stronger. She needed to regain her strength quickly. That was why she was napping in the middle of the day and letting Paul boss her around. That and the fact that she was worn-out.

A knock on the door had her yelping and scooting under the blanket. "Come in," she called as the door opened.

"We're here to kiss you," Suzanne announced as if Roz could have possibly forgotten. Suzanne released Paul's hand and scampered across the room, giving Roz a rare glimpse of the happy child she'd once been.

"I'm ready."

Suzanne leaned over and wrapped her arms around Roz's neck. She pecked Roz's cheek, leaving the stickiness of peanut butter and jelly behind. "Have sweet dreams, Mommy."

"Thank you."

Suzanne moved aside. "Your turn, Uncle Paul."

Roz's heart pounded as she watched Paul's long legs eat up the distance between them. His eyes were riveted on her face and she couldn't look away to save her life. As he got closer, warmth bloomed in her stomach and tingles shot to her fingers and toes. He just stood there, staring at her.

"Kiss her," Suzanne prodded.

"Right." He leaned over, placing a hand on either side of her head, imprisoning her. Ever so slowly, he moved closer until she thought her heart would burst from her chest. His masculine scent, a combination of soap and aftershave, surrounded her, and she yearned to turn her face toward him and capture his kiss with her lips. Instead, she lay frozen as he brushed his lips against her cheek. For a moment, the years dropped away and they were young and in love again. She forced that thought away.

The past was over and there was no getting back what they'd lost. She'd blown her chance years ago. Looking back, she realized she'd made a mistake, but she'd been alone and afraid, in need of someone to hold on to. Paul hadn't understood how scared she'd been. He still didn't. At least he no longer hated her. Over the past few months they'd become friends. Family even. That would have to be enough.

Chapter Eleven

Paul stepped into the hallway and slumped against the wall, fighting to remain upright. Swiping his suddenly damp forehead with his wrist, he blew out a shaky breath. What the hell was wrong with him? It was just a simple kiss, and really hardly that. His lips had barely touched her cheek before he pulled away. Despite the fact that Suzanne had leaned in close to make sure he kissed Roz as directed, and despite the fact that Roz lay as still as a stone, the kiss had nearly brought him to his knees. Even now, his lips still tingled.

She smelled so good. Roz had never been a big fan of perfume because it always made her sneeze.

To him, she hadn't needed it. He'd always found her unique scent intoxicating. Since his arrival over three months ago, he'd seen her in varying stages of undress and hadn't been the least bit aroused. So why was he noticing how very soft her skin was now? Or the way her breath caught in her throat when he kissed her? There was only one explanation. He had holes in his head and his common sense had leaked out.

Living in the same house with Roz was twisting his thinking and dulling the memory of the pain she'd caused him. It was as if the past years hadn't happened or someone else had suffered through the agony of loving and losing her. He couldn't let himself forget what she'd done. He couldn't set himself up for more pain.

He needed to get out of here before his weakening will got the better of him and he did something stupid like go back into her room and kiss her the way he was aching to.

He managed to regain his composure before he walked into the living room. Nathaniel was sprawled on the floor reading a comic book. Megan and Suzanne were doing paint by number pictures at the coffee table.

"I need to go out," he said to Charlotte, who was flipping through a bridal magazine. She'd made herself scarce during Roz's reunion with the kids. Thank goodness she hadn't left yet. "Can you stay a while longer?"

"Sure. Rick and Bobby are coming to get Nathaniel so they can go to the park for a while. The girls and I will be fine here, so take your time."

"I won't be gone more than an hour." That should be long enough to clear all thoughts of Roz from his mind. He gently tugged Megan's and Suzanne's braids. "I'll see you girls later."

"Bye," Suzanne said without glancing up from her picture.

Megan stood and stretched out her arms, reaching for him. He bent over and she grabbed his face with her little hands then placed a sloppy kiss on his cheek. "Bye, Uncle Paul."

Paul jogged down the porch steps and to his car. He didn't have any destination in mind, so he just drove aimlessly, using the time to rebuild the emotional wall he needed to keep between himself and Roz. He turned on the radio to his favorite oldies station. His mother always joked that he'd been born too late. He liked the Platters, the Rat Pack and doo-wop. Nothing pulled him out of a funk faster than a song with a good melody and catchy lyrics.

Now he was so unsettled that the music lacked its usual magic. Driving down Main Street, he passed the mayor, Lex Devlin. Although Paul hadn't spent a lot of time with the other man, he counted Lex as a new friend, so he waved and pulled over, lowering the passenger window.

"Everything okay?" Lex asked, leaning against the car.

"Sure. Why do you ask?"

"I know you picked up Roz from the hospital today. How did her surgery go?"

"The doctor is cautiously optimistic. Whatever that means."

Lex shrugged. Apparently he didn't speak medicalese any more fluently than Paul did. He was going to ask Rick to translate when he brought Nathaniel home that afternoon.

"Where are you going?"

"Nowhere in particular. You?"

"I'm about to grab a burger. Want to join me?"

Paul nodded and parked. They walked the half block to Mabel's Diner and found an empty booth. After they ordered, Lex looked at him. Although the mayor didn't speak, Paul could tell he had something on his mind.

"What?" Paul asked.

"Now that Roz has had her surgery, I wonder what your plans are."

"I haven't thought that far ahead. To be honest, I haven't thought past today. She still has a long recovery ahead of her. Why?"

"I have a business proposition for you."

Talking about business was preferable to discussing Roz's illness, which made him queasy. "Shoot."

"Sweet Briar is the perfect place for a health club."

"Sweet Briar?"

"Don't sell us short. I'm not just blowing smoke. I've done my research. I've visited several of your clubs and know the clientele you serve. There's no place within an hour in any direction that has the amenities you offer. You can attract people from the surrounding areas who aren't being served right now. You could do nicely here."

Paul agreed Sweet Briar could be a prime location for one of his clubs. He'd actually considered the idea before tossing it aside. He didn't want anything to tie him to Roz. Though headquartered in Florida, he prioritized the time he devoted to new locations. He always stuck around for the first few weeks and made frequent visits in the months following the opening to insure everything stayed true to his vision. Experience taught him that it was easier to nip a bad habit in the bud than to break it after it had become ingrained. Though he had trusted employees, his name and reputation were on the line. If he opened a club here, he'd have to make regular visits to Sweet Briar forever. He'd never break free of Roz if he kept seeing her.

Fortunately, Lex didn't pursue the conversation further. That was one of the reasons Lex was such a popular and successful mayor. He didn't pressure anyone to commit to something they might later regret. He made offers and let people make their own decisions in their own time.

Their food arrived and they switched topics once more, talking about sports, and Paul was able to enjoy his meal.

Paul pondered Lex's suggestion as he drove the short distance home. He blinked. It wasn't his home. He couldn't allow himself to think of Roz's house that way. That would lead him down a dangerous road he had no desire to travel. But despite his resistance, he'd already taken a few steps on that path.

He'd already grown attached to her kids and loved them as if they were his own. It would be easy to pretend they were. But he couldn't pretend away the past. The past had happened and it had been soul crushing. No man in his right mind would put his heart in Roz's hands again and trust her not to break it.

The sound of a singing Disney princess greeted him when he stepped into the house. Megan and Suzanne were huddled together on the sofa. Suzanne had her thumb in her mouth. She looked up, pulled her thumb from her mouth, and smiled before turning back to the movie.

He found Charlotte in the kitchen, taking one of the endless casseroles the townspeople had delivered from the freezer. She raised the dish. "Dinner?"

He didn't think the kids could choke down another casserole. He knew he couldn't. "No. I'll cook something."

She shoved the pan back into the freezer. "In that case, I'll head on out."

"Thanks for all of your help. I couldn't have managed all these months without you."

She tilted her head quizzically, as though she might say something. Charlotte wasn't known for holding her tongue. Instead, she smiled and left, taking her unspoken comment with her.

Giving in to the need to check on Roz, he opened her door and peered inside. She was lying on her side, her head resting on her hands. She looked so serene. He felt himself being drawn farther into the room, closer to her. When he reached her side, he straightened the blankets and pulled the fabric over her narrow shoulders. He told himself to leave but couldn't make his feet obey. Sighing, he sat down beside her, allowing himself a moment to just be with her. His heart felt calmer than it had since she'd told him about her cancer diagnosis. More at peace than he'd felt in years. But his heart wasn't his brain. He needed to think with the correct organ this time.

Her eyes opened and she smiled. Stretched. "How long have I been sleeping?"

"Not long. A couple of hours."

She pushed herself into a sitting position, then leaned against the headboard. "I guess I should get up. I need to warm up one of those casseroles."

He raised a hand. "I'll handle dinner."

"I need to get back to taking care of my family." If she was trying to sound fierce, the yawn ruined the effect.

"I know. And you will. Just not tonight. I'd appreciate it if you help the girls set the table."

"I can do that."

"Good. I'll put a star on your chart."

She brushed a hand over her head then reached for her scarf. As a teenager, her thick hair had hung between her shoulder blades. She'd cut it a few inches since then, but until the chemo, it had been just as thick. Just as beautiful.

Roz noticed where he was looking and knotted the scarf. "I must look like death warmed over. As I've told you before, sometimes I look in the mirror and scare myself. I don't recognize the person looking back at me."

He knew she wasn't mourning a loss of beauty. She was just as gorgeous as ever. To him, her hair loss was a reminder of the battle she was fighting. And though she had her flaws, vanity wasn't one of them. "It's only hair. It'll grow back."

The grateful smile she gave him was radiant, and he backed away, trying to evade its warmth. The heat reached him anyway and soothed aches in his heart the way the passage of time had failed to do. No matter how hard he struggled, he was getting pulled into her orbit again. He had to fight harder to fortify the walls around his heart. He wished he could let her in, but he couldn't. The thought didn't make him happy, but that was the way it had to be.

Roz placed the last knife on a napkin then stood back to admire the dining room table. It looked pretty good, if she did say so herself. They didn't ordinarily set the table so fancy. In fact, they generally didn't eat in the dining room. Before she'd gotten sick, she'd fill the kids' plates at the stove and they'd carry them to the kitchen table. But Paul had insisted this was a celebration—this was the one-week anniversary of her release from the hospital—and the kids had sided with him. Their enthusiasm was contagious and she'd gotten into the spirit, using the special dishes and good silverware. They were even using cloth napkins and a tablecloth. Maybe that was overdoing it a bit, but it would be worth it if it made her kids smile.

The aromas floating from the kitchen were heavenly, and her stomach growled as her long-suppressed appetite made a surprise appearance. She turned on some music and shimmied a little to the beat. The sound of Paul's laughter had her cheeks warming as she spun around. He was holding a bouquet of fall flowers. The rich oranges, deep reds and vibrant yellows made a stunning combination.

"I thought you were in the kitchen," she said.

"The girls insisted that we needed flowers to

make the table pretty, so I left Nathaniel in charge while I ran out to the florist."

"They're beautiful." She'd told him long ago that these were her favorite flowers, but surely this was a coincidence. There was no way he remembered her preference after all these years.

"If I would have known I was missing a dance party, I would have come home sooner."

"Oh, you never know what you miss when you're not around." She shook her shoulders playfully and he laughed again.

He set the flowers on the table and wiggled his hips in a silly motion that should have looked ridiculous, but instead it was…hot.

They danced lightheartedly to the music for a few moments. Then the upbeat song ended and a slow song replaced it. Mere inches away, Paul held out a hand to her. She should have resisted, but she was having too much fun to stop, so she took his hand and let him draw her into his arms.

Sighing, she leaned her head against his shoulder as they moved together, listening to the baritone sing about love at first sight. Paul's heartbeat was steady beneath her ear and her heart pounded in time with his. Nothing could feel better than being held in Paul's strong arms, breathing in his masculine scent with every breath she took.

When the song ended, they didn't move. His hands remained on her waist and she kept hers draped around his neck. She lifted her face and their eyes met. Held. Time froze. Ever so slowly, he lowered his head. Their lips were only inches apart when Megan burst into the room.

“Is it time to eat yet? I’m hungry,” Megan said, hopping on one foot. Suzanne trailed behind her sister, her thumb in her mouth.

“Absolutely,” Paul said, stepping away from Roz and leaving her yearning for the missed kiss. If only her kids had waited a few more seconds before they’d come into the room. If only. Those had to be the two saddest words she knew. “Why don’t you ladies sit down and Nathaniel and I will bring in the food.”

“We’re not ladies, we’re girls,” Megan corrected. “Mommy is a lady.”

“Right,” Paul said, pulling out the girls’ chairs. Roz made a move to pull out her chair, hoping to mask her disappointment about the missed opportunity. Paul placed his hand on hers, stopping her. The warmth of his skin practically scorched her hand, yet she didn’t want to pull away. “Let me.”

Their eyes met and a shiver traveled down her spine at the emotion she saw there. Maybe he was longing for the missed kiss, too. “Thanks,” she whispered.

He nodded, then disappeared into the kitchen.

Moments later, he emerged carrying a rotisserie chicken on a platter. Nathaniel followed with a dish filled with roasted red potatoes. After two more trips, the table overflowed with Roz's favorite foods. Nathaniel and Paul were taking their seats when Megan burst out. "We forgot the candles, Uncle Paul."

"Right. I'll get them."

"I'll turn out the lights," Nathaniel said. "Then it will be perfect."

Paul placed two crystal candlesticks on either side of the flowers then lit the wicks. At his nod, Nathaniel switched off the lights.

Despite the fact that her children were present, the image was romantic enough to give her chills.

"Ooh, pretty," Megan said, clapping her hands.

"Are we going to sing 'Happy Birthday'?" Suzanne asked.

"No, baby," Paul said. "The candles are to make the table look prettier."

"When are we going to blow them out and turn the lights back on?"

"After we eat," Nathaniel said.

"How will we see our food?" Suzanne persisted.

"Too dark?" Paul asked.

She nodded.

Paul strode to the windows and opened the blinds, letting in the fading sunlight. "Better?"

Suzanne smiled at him, hero worship written on her face. "Better."

Paul returned to the table, and, after leading them in grace, served the food. Roz sampled everything, then smiled at her family. "This is delicious. Thank you so much."

"I put the almonds in the string beans," Megan boasted. "And I put the butter on the rolls."

"I made the potatoes and the chocolate cake," Nathaniel added.

"I didn't do anything important," Suzanne said sadly.

"Of course you did. You kept us all company," Paul said. "That's very important. No one wants to be alone in the kitchen."

"And you thought of the flowers," Nathaniel added.

"See," Roz said. "You were very important."

Suzanne beamed. "I like being important."

Roz and Paul were seated at opposite ends of the table, the kids on either side. Whenever she looked up, she was treated to a view of his face. He led the children in conversation, encouraging them to tell Roz what they'd done in school that day. It was clear that he'd made himself a part of her family. Although she was glad her kids had come to love him, she didn't want their hearts to be broken when he left. Sadly, she didn't know how to protect any of their hearts, including hers.

"You need to sit down. Nathaniel and I can clean up."

Roz added two glasses to the dishwasher, then

leaned against the counter. "I can handle it, Paul. You guys cooked so it's only right that I help clean the kitchen."

"Sounds fair to me," Nathaniel said, edging out the door.

"Freeze." Paul glared at his nephew, then pointed at the broom. "Sweep."

Nathaniel grabbed the broom and began sweeping as if trying to set a speed record. After he dumped the debris into the garbage can, he leaned the broom against a wall and raced into the front room to watch television with his sisters. That left Paul alone with Roz.

Despite knowing that he was walking on dangerous ground, he couldn't keep his eyes from straying to her whenever he thought she wasn't looking. At the moment, she was bent over the dishwasher, filling the lower level with plates and humming a vaguely familiar melody. He stepped closer, bringing the last of the dirty dishes. She chose that moment to stand, bumping into him as she did so. She was knocked off balance, so he placed a hand on her waist to steady her.

A faint tingle buzzed over his fingertips. For the second time that day, he'd been aroused by a simple touch, and the desire to kiss her nearly overwhelmed him. This time, he couldn't count on one of the kids providing him with a timely interruption. Not when coming into the kitchen might result in being put to work.

And what about Kristin? Though he'd stopped calling her since she hadn't returned even one of his messages, he still thought they had a chance to make their relationship work. Or was he just clinging to that belief as a way to keep Roz at bay? Was he using Kristin as a barrier between him and Roz? Probably. Maybe he should stop doing that and see where his feelings led, but he wasn't ready to do that yet. He needed to think before jumping into the fire. He had to be sure he knew what he was doing and that his feelings were real. Right now his head wasn't clear and he was too busy to think straight. So he couldn't act. It would be wrong to give Roz the wrong impression or lead her on.

He cleared his throat. "About earlier. I want to apologize for my behavior."

"That's not necessary. We both just got swept up in the moment. This has been a stressful time for all of us and our emotions are all over the place. We were just releasing some of the tension."

Was she giving him an easy out or did she really mean what she said? "Is that what you think it was?"

"Of course. I know you're seeing someone. I'm not the type to try and come between the two of you. I hope you know that."

"I do." It was clear to him that she was worried

he might think the worst of her. "Actually, Kristin and I are no longer seeing each other."

"Since when?"

He blew out a breath then led her to the table. "She didn't want me coming here."

"I'm sorry, Paul. I didn't think of what asking you to come here would cost you. Maybe you should have gone home a while ago. You're free to go now. Maybe you and Kristin can reconcile. I can handle it from here."

No, she couldn't. She'd had major surgery a little over a week ago and had restrictions on her activities. And she was still occasionally weak from chemotherapy, although not nearly as often or severe as before. She might be able to do most things for herself, but there was no way she could care for three kids, even with the help of Charlotte and her other friends. She still needed him. He'd made a commitment to her and he intended to keep it. "I'm not going anywhere."

"Then call her. Maybe if you talk to her, she'll understand. I'll talk to her if you think that will help."

"She doesn't pick up when I call and she hasn't returned any of my messages. She's ignored my texts and emails. It's over."

"Sorry. I know how that feels."

"What do you mean?"

"That's what happened when you went away to school. I tried to keep in touch with you, but I felt you pulling away. After a while, I figured that we were through and that you expected me to get the hint. That's why I never told you when Terrence started coming around. I didn't think you'd care. I'm sorry for hurting you. That was never my intention." She stood. "I'm going to watch TV with the kids awhile. I know you don't want my advice, but I'm going to give it to you anyway. If you still have feelings for Kristin, call her. Don't let a misunderstanding cost you a relationship you want. If you do, you'll regret it forever."

Paul pondered Roz's words long after she and the kids had gone to bed. For the first time in years, he actually saw things from her point of view. Now he realized that she hadn't owed him an apology. He'd owed her one. Because, though she'd broken his heart, he'd broken hers first.

He and Roz had been kids when they'd sworn to love each other forever. She'd been seventeen and he'd been eighteen. How many high school kids made vows like that with the best of intentions, only to realize they hadn't been as deeply in love as they had believed? That didn't make them bad people. That just made them young.

Looking back, it was understandable that she would take his silence as rejection. She hadn't had a serious boyfriend until he came along. He'd promised to always be there for her. To always love her. And then he'd left. Not long after, her aunt died and she was all alone. Was it all that surprising that she turned to Terrence and the security he represented? Nothing was black-and-white, as he'd always believed.

Paul had intended to keep in contact with her, but he hadn't. He'd thought about her all the time, but she had no way of knowing that. His actions were all she had to go by. In retrospect, it was easy to see how she'd come to believe that he'd stopped caring. That hadn't been the case. His classwork had been more time-consuming than he'd expected. He'd also participated in a lot of extracurricular activities. Roz had remained in his heart and he'd loved her as much as ever. But how was she supposed to know that if she didn't hear from him for days on end?

Sure, he wished she would have had more faith in him, but he should have done more to deserve that faith. Who knew if they would have made a relationship work long-term? And really, did it matter now? Twelve years had passed and they'd gone on with their lives.

It was time to let go of the past for real. Especially since he wasn't blameless. Roz had let him down, but he'd let her down first. All this time, he'd been sure he couldn't trust her with his heart. The reality was that she hadn't been able to trust him with hers.

Chapter Twelve

Roz watched out the kitchen window as Paul and the kids worked on the lawn. The weather was cool and the leaves had begun falling from the trees. Roz had spent the past week welcoming the change of season as her strength slowly returned. She didn't quite have the energy she'd once had, but she wasn't as exhausted as she'd been either. Three weeks after surgery, she was starting to believe that she might actually make a full recovery. Oh, she knew there were more tests to be had in the months and years to come, but she was making headway on the road to wellness.

Paul and Nathaniel had raked the leaves into a

big pile and, one by one, the kids ran and jumped into them. Their laughter was a balm to her soul. They'd been outside quite a while and the chicken and dumplings she'd made for dinner were about ten minutes from being done, but she didn't call them in right away. They were having such fun, she didn't want to make them stop. It had been so long since they'd been carefree. She wanted them to enjoy as many special times as they could. A few minutes more wouldn't ruin anything.

Humming to herself, she grabbed a gallon of apple cider. She'd warm it and add cinnamon sticks, making one of their favorite beverages to drink on fall days. It had been unseasonably cold over the past week, but Roz had no complaints. She liked snuggling with her kids to read or watch one of their favorite shows on television. She and the girls had become addicted to jigsaw puzzles and spent many hours working on them. They'd glued and framed two puzzles, which now hung on the girls' bedroom wall.

She was setting the table when the kitchen door opened and everyone rushed inside. Noise and laughter filled the room.

"Is dinner ready?" Nathaniel asked.

"Yep. Wash your hands and sit down."

The kids ran out and she was left alone with Paul, who washed his hands at the kitchen sink. Over the past few days, he'd spent many hours working outside, getting the house ready for winter. He'd fertilized the lawn and shaped the bushes. He'd also washed the windows and repainted the porch, stairs and trim. The house looked so good that Megan and Suzanne said it looked like a princess house. Roz appreciated all that he was doing for her, but she was worried he was wearing himself out. Of course, she wouldn't tell him to slow down. She hadn't appreciated it when he'd tried to tell her what to do, so she wouldn't give him unsolicited advice either.

The kids raced back in and took their chairs at the table. Megan and Nathaniel chattered away as usual, and Suzanne took part in the conversation. Paul was quieter than usual, and Roz wondered if he was already mentally removing himself from their family. Perhaps he'd been working overtime to get the house into shape so that he could leave them behind with a clear conscience.

He'd gone above and beyond for her family. Roz wished she could do something for him in return. But since he didn't need anything from her, she would always be in his debt.

They finished dinner and dessert and the kids went to their rooms to play while Roz and Paul cleaned the kitchen.

"Penny for your thoughts," Paul said, leaning back against his chair.

"That's all? You can't get much for a penny these days."

"True enough. How about a dollar?"

Roz laughed. "I guess that's a fair enough price. I wasn't really thinking about anything. Just enjoying the quiet before I go to bed."

"They sure did go out fast," Paul said. When they'd gone upstairs to check on the kids, they'd found them already asleep so they'd returned to the kitchen for a nightcap.

"That just means they'll be up earlier tomorrow." Roz covered her mouth as she yawned.

"Looks like they're not the only ones ready for bed."

"I hate that I still tire so easily."

"You've come so far, Roz. Don't rush things."

She frowned. "That's easy for you to say. You aren't the one who was dependent on someone else for months on end. You aren't the one who couldn't take care of your own family."

"I know," he said softly, surprising her. She'd half expected him to snap as she had. "But you've made great progress. You're getting stronger every day. Your appetite is better and you aren't taking as many naps as before."

"You're right. I know that. It's just that..." Her voice trailed off.

"Just that what?"

She hesitated. She'd never told him how things had been growing up. As a teen, she'd been too embarrassed. Now, though, she needed him to understand where she was coming from. "This isn't the first time I've been in this situation. My parents died when I was five, remember?"

"Of course I remember. You went to live with your aunt."

"Yes. But the truth is..." She blew out a breath. Why was it so hard to say the words after all this time? "My aunt didn't want me."

"What do you mean? You lived with her most of your life."

"And she hated every minute of it. She'd liked being single and living her own life. Before I came to live with her, Aunt Rosemary traveled a lot. She did her 'own thing,' as she liked to call it. When my parents died, she took me in, but she never for a moment let me forget that I'd changed her life in a way she didn't like. I tried to be as quiet as I could and not make trouble. I cleaned the house and basically tried to be invisible."

His eyes filled with sadness as the truth dawned on him. "That's why we never hung out at your house."

"I liked being outside anyway, which was good, but yes. I was an obligation. A responsibility. That's kind of the way I felt when I had to come to you for help."

"You weren't just an obligation to me, Roz."

"Then what was I?"

He stared at his hands for a long time. When he

looked up at her, his eyes were shadowed and she couldn't decipher the emotion there. "I don't know. I didn't come only because I felt obligated. I came because you needed me."

Roz noticed that he didn't say he hadn't felt obligated, just that obligation hadn't been the only motivating factor. It was better than nothing, she supposed.

They sat for a while, neither of them speaking. Finally, Roz stood. "I guess I'll go to bed. Good night. See you in the morning."

Paul sat in the dark, pondering Roz's words. He'd loved her all those years ago, but he hadn't known anything about her. Sure he knew her favorite flowers, but none of the really important things. He'd never thought of what her life must have been like, living with her great-aunt. Not once had he considered how her aunt would treat a five-year-old who'd upended her life. Now that he knew, he understood how desperate she must have been to have come to him for help. At least she'd had the peace of mind that came with being in her own home. She wasn't an outsider here. He was. Yet she'd never made him feel that way. She'd always made him feel welcome. At home.

He should go to bed, but he was glued to the chair. Twenty minutes had passed since Roz had left the room, yet her scent still lingered in the air. Her bedroom was next to the kitchen, so, for several minutes, he heard her moving around as she took off her clothes and then slipped on her nightgown.

He pictured her sitting on the edge of the bed, rubbing lotion on her hands and feet, keeping her skin as soft as a baby's.

He couldn't leave this room as long as the image of her was at the forefront of his mind. He wasn't sure whether he would go up the stairs to his bedroom, or across the room to hers.

He dragged a hand down his face. Nothing made sense. He wasn't in love with Roz anymore. He hadn't been for years. Yet there was something about her that drew him. He was like a fish caught on a hook. Fate had allowed him plenty of line, letting him swim away as if he were free, then snatching him back. Something kept pulling him back to Roz and he was unable to untangle himself. Even more confusing, he wasn't sure he wanted to be free. As crazy as it seemed, he liked having her in his life again.

Paul inhaled deeply and blew the breath from his nose, too tired to try to sort out his feelings for Roz. Morning came fast when you lived with little kids. The girls were at an age when they woke up early. Though Suzanne was quiet, Megan was fully charged, and both were ready to eat. They didn't differentiate between school days, vacation days or weekends. It was "up and at 'em." At eleven,

Nathaniel appreciated the beauty of sleeping late. Paul, like his nephew, liked to ease into his day. Unfortunately, unlike Nathaniel, Paul no longer had that luxury. Tomorrow might be Sunday, but he still would have to get up early.

After checking that the doors and windows were locked, he climbed the stairs and got into bed. Barely a minute had passed when he felt his right eye being pried open.

"Suzanne, stop that." Nathaniel's voice.

Paul's eyelid dropped over his eye again and he struggled to open both eyes. Obviously, he'd slept longer than he'd intended if Nathaniel was already awake. Odd, since he still felt tired. He finally managed to open his eyes, then tried to push himself into a sitting position but was too exhausted to pull it off. Why was he so weak and out of breath?

"Mom, he's awake," Nathaniel bellowed, making Paul's already pounding headache hurt even more.

"Coming," Roz replied. Her voice sounded far away.

"You slept a long time," Megan said from her position at the foot of his bed. She was looking at him as if not sure what to think.

"I didn't think you were ever going to wake up," Suzanne said in a tiny voice.

Despite feeling like a truck had driven over him while he slept, he reached out a hand for the little girl, surprised at the effort it took to raise his arm. "I guess the sandman dropped a little extra sand in my eyes last night." They felt so gritty that there might be a beach in there.

"Who is the sandman, and why would he put sand in your eyes? That's mean. Did he break into the house while we were sleeping?" Suzanne asked, looking frightened. He'd forgotten how literal she was. Great. He'd given her something else to worry about.

"The sandman is a pretend person," Roz said, coming through the door. Dressed in a yellow top and denim skirt, she outshone the sun, and his sore eyes definitely appreciated the sight. "Kind of like the three pigs. In his story, he puts sand in people's eyes to help them fall asleep at night."

"So he's not a bad man?" Megan asked. Obviously, the idea of putting sand in someone's eyes didn't sound like a good thing to her. To be honest, it didn't sound good to him either.

"He's not a bad man," Roz confirmed.

"I don't want sand in my eyes," Suzanne said.

"Good, since nobody is going to put any in there," Roz said, tugging on her daughter's braid. Roz looked at him and smiled and his aches temporarily vanished. "Why don't you run along so I can talk to Uncle Paul?"

"Okay. Bye, Uncle Paul," the girls cried as they ran from the room.

He tried to respond but suffered a sudden coughing fit.

"I'll get the cough medicine," Nathaniel offered.

"Thanks," Roz said, stepping closer to Paul's bed. "Looks like someone has come down with the flu."

"No way. I'm never sick."

"No? You do a pretty good imitation." She reached out and touched his forehead with the back of her hand. It was so cool. So soft. So arousing. "You feel warm."

"Hot is more like it."

She raised her eyebrow at his double entendre but otherwise remained silent. Good, because for the life of him he couldn't think of a way to make that statement sound purely innocent. Which proved her point. If he couldn't think on his feet, even lying flat on his back, he had to be sick.

"Let me take your temperature." She reached out and he grabbed her wrist before she could touch him again.

"That's not a good idea."

She shook her hand free. "Why not? The thermometer goes in your ear and only takes a second."

"You shouldn't even be in here."

"Why not?"

"Because I'm sick and you're vulnerable to me."

"You think I'm going to fall head over heels in love with you because your eyes are glazed and you're covered with sweat? I think I can manage to contain myself. We need to get you another T-shirt by the way. That one is drenched."

"Don't be dense. You know what I'm talking about."

"Actually, I don't think anyone knows what you're talking about, including you."

He suffered another coughing fit before talking. "I'm contagious. And you're compromised."

She wrinkled her brow in confusion. Finally, she smiled. "My immunity is compromised, you mean."

He nodded. He must have rocks in his head, because they banged around, making his head hurt even more. "Right. I don't want you coming in here. You'll make yourself sick."

"I'm no longer undergoing chemo. I haven't had a cycle since before the surgery. It's out of my system. It's perfectly safe for me to take care of you."

"I'm not your responsibility, Roz."

"And I'm not yours either, Paul."

"Of course you are. That's why I'm here. You need me to take care of you."

Her eyes narrowed and he could practically see lightning bolts shooting from them. Had he just compared her to the sun? She was more like an atomic bomb, ready to incinerate him.

"I don't need you to take care of me. Not anymore. I'm stronger now."

"Go away and leave me alone. Don't touch me. If you do, I'll never be able to leave."

Roz gasped and stepped back. The pain in her eyes had him replaying what he'd just said. The jumbled words didn't accurately reflect what he was thinking. But his head was muddled and the connection between his brain and mouth had short-circuited. Her hand on his skin felt so good he could barely resist her. If he let her continue to touch him, it would be harder to walk away from her. And he needed to walk away, if only for the time it took to figure out how he felt and to focus on his business.

"Fine. You win. I'm out of here. You can hack up a lung for all I care." She spun and brushed past Nathaniel, who was standing just inside the door, holding a bottle of cough medicine and a spoon. Paul hoped Nathaniel hadn't heard the conversation.

"Do you want this or not?" Nathaniel snapped. Yep. He'd heard. And he hadn't liked the way Paul had spoken to his mother.

Paul heaved out an achy breath. "Please."

Nathaniel crossed the floor and handed over the bottle and spoon. Paul squeezed the top and twisted. Nothing. The top didn't budge. He must be sicker than he thought if he couldn't even open a bottle. Sighing, Nathaniel snatched the bottle, opened it and poured medicine onto the spoon. For a moment, Paul thought the kid was going to tell him to open wide and shove the spoon down his throat. Instead, his nephew handed him the spoon, watched him swallow the cough syrup, repeated the process, then turned to walk away.

"Wait." Paul couldn't let Nathaniel's anger fester. Paul was discovering that doing so hurt everyone, including innocent bystanders. Besides, he owed his nephew an apology. Nathaniel turned back around, his young face marred by anger. Nathaniel was protective of his family. Paul mustered his energy and scooted to the center of the bed. "Sit down a minute. Please."

Too well-raised to disobey, Nathaniel frowned and sat on the very edge of the bed. His eyes conveyed the angry words he wouldn't say.

"I'm sorry. I shouldn't have spoken to your mother like that."

"You should be telling her that."

"I will. That is, if she ever steps foot in this room again."

"She will. Mom can't stay mad at anyone for long."

Not like Paul, who could hold a grudge like it had a handle dipped in superglue. He needed to work on changing that. "I also want to apologize to you. I shouldn't have disrespected your mother. Or you. Being sick isn't much of an excuse, but it's all that I have."

Nathaniel nodded. "I get mean when I don't feel good, too. A lot of people do. Well, not Mom. She never gets mean about anything."

"No. She doesn't." It wasn't anger he'd seen on her face when she'd fled the room. It was pain. Sorrow instead of fury. And humiliation. All because he'd gotten his thoughts muddled, saying only part of what he was thinking and none of what he meant.

"And, Uncle Paul, I'll take care of you. That way Mom won't get sick again. I hate it when she's sick." He leaned in closer, his voice a near whisper although the two of them were alone. "Don't tell anybody, but I was a little scared, too."

"I know." For all his maturity, Nathaniel still was a little boy who'd lost his father and needed his mother.

Paul was about to say that he didn't need much help when he began to cough. Not only that, but he was suddenly chilled and began to shiver. The fresh T-shirt that Roz had mentioned was starting to sound good. As hard as it was for him to accept, he did need help.

Once he could talk again, he asked Nathaniel to bring him the shirt, which Nathaniel quickly fetched.

"Thanks." After changing his shirt and swallowing some orange juice, Paul sank under the blanket and closed his eyes. He'd find a way to apologize to Roz later when he wasn't so tired. Or contagious.

"Are you sure that bad man won't put sand in my eyes?" Suzanne asked for the umpteenth time. She was fighting as hard as she could to stay awake.

Every time Roz thought she'd gotten her daughter to fall asleep, her eyes would pop open and she'd look around the room, frantically searching for the bad man.

"I promise. Remember, he's only make-believe, like the three bears. And he only helps people who can't fall asleep." Roz rubbed Suzanne's back as she'd done when she'd been a baby and needed soothing.

Suzanne didn't answer and her eyes stayed closed. Thank goodness. Who would have thought an innocent comment would cause this much worry? Suzanne's reaction wouldn't be so troubling if she weren't already so stressed.

Not that Suzanne was the only one being pushed to the emotional edge. They all were teetering on the brink. The effects of the past months hadn't dissipated simply because she was feeling better. If they weren't careful, the stress would bubble over into every area of their lives. She needed to find a way to turn down the heat. If she didn't, a big explosion was on the horizon, with the potential to blow their lives apart.

Speaking of explosions, she stepped out of the room, closed the door behind her, then headed across the hall to Paul's room. She'd avoided him all day, letting Nathaniel take care of him. Well, Nathaniel was the one who'd entered the room. But Roz had cooked the chicken soup and filled pitchers of water and glasses of orange juice throughout the day. She'd been the one to tell Nathaniel when it was time to give Paul another dose of medicine. Nathaniel was asleep now, so it was up to her to make sure that Paul had everything he needed for the night. If he wasn't too stubborn, she'd change the sheets. They had to be damp by now. Nothing felt better than lying on clean sheets when you were sick.

She knocked on the door and he coughed in reply. Interpreting that as an invitation to enter, she stepped inside. He was lying in bed, looking pitiful. Despite her intention to keep her feelings protected, her heart ached for him. Misery filled his red-rimmed eyes. The blankets were twisted around his body in a way that couldn't possibly be comfortable. Crumpled tissues overflowed the garbage can and several tissues dotted the floor nearby.

He raised his hand as if that could keep her out. She would have snapped at him if she didn't know his reluctance to have her around stemmed from his genuine concern for her health.

"I checked with my doctor," she said, standing just inside the door. "Like I told you earlier, I'm not at risk. But since I know you won't be satisfied, I've got gloves. And a mask. Okay?"

In the midst of a coughing fit, he nodded.

She donned the gloves and covered her mouth and nose before she approached him. By that time, he'd managed to stop coughing. "When was the last time you took some cough medicine?"

He shrugged and her eyes were immediately drawn to his massive shoulders. His T-shirt was drenched and clung to his sculpted muscles. There was a time when she had the right to run her hands over that torso, but that was no longer the case. Chiding herself for ogling him when he was obviously uncomfortable, she forced her eyes away from his chest and looked into his eyes. Even drowsy with sickness, she feared they could see to her very soul. Thank goodness it wasn't her soul that was filled with longing.

"Can you guess?" she asked, trying to get back on track. She'd told Nathaniel when to bring in the medicine, but that didn't mean Paul had actually taken it.

"What time is it now?"

"Nine thirty."

"About five hours, I think."

"Time for more." She grabbed the bottle and dug through the pile of discarded tissue and dishes to find the spoon. "I'll be right back."

She stacked the bowls and glasses, then walked to the door, aware that his eyes followed her every move. Grateful for the years spent waitressing in high school, she managed to move without dropping anything. In the kitchen, she quickly rinsed the dishes and put them into the dishwasher. Her nerves jumped up and down, trying to draw her attention, which was ridiculous. She was so over Paul. Okay, that was a lie, but a necessary one. Because she knew he was so over her.

She grabbed a clean spoon and returned to Paul's room. He'd stopped coughing and was now propped against the headboard, two pillows behind his back. She filled the spoon with medicine and offered it to him. Instead of taking it, he leaned forward, his eyes locked with hers, and closed his mouth around the spoon. Mesmerized, she watched his lips as he pulled back.

She let her arm drop to her side and tried to slow her rapidly beating heart. Caring for a sick man shouldn't be this hard. And it definitely shouldn't turn her on. If she didn't want to waste time pining for Paul after he left, she needed to stunt her growing attraction.

And he was ready to go. He'd been unequivocal about that. He was probably counting the minutes until he could return to Florida. He might even try to reignite his relationship with Kristin. Now that Paul wouldn't be living in Sweet Briar, Kristin might be inclined to take him back. Regardless of what happened between Paul and Kristin, it was in Roz's best interest to get her feelings under control so she could avoid heartbreak.

"If you want, I can change your sheets," she offered.

He looked conflicted. Clearly he wanted fresh sheets but didn't want her to overdo it. Perhaps he thought she would keel over from the effort. She mentally rolled her eyes and waited for his reply.

"I do," he finally admitted, "but I don't think I can stand up long enough for you to change them."

So it wasn't about her at all. She'd totally misinterpreted his silence. "I have three children. I've perfected the art of changing sheets with someone in the bed."

"In that case, thanks."

She hurried to the linen closet and grabbed clean sheets, pillowcases and two fresh blankets, and returned to his room.

Paul looked at her. "What do you need me to do?"

"Nothing. Just stay where you are." She crossed to the far side of the bed and loosened the soiled sheets, then pulled on the clean ones, tightening them at the head and foot of the bed. After pushing aside the old sheets, she smoothed the new ones across the mattress until she was practically touching Paul.

He groaned and she spun around. "Are you okay?"

He nodded. "Just a little bit achy."

"Now scoot over onto the new sheet."

Paul complied and she removed the soiled sheet and then pulled the clean sheet tight over the mattress. She quickly added the top sheet and blankets.

"That's some trick," Paul said.

"I've got mad skills," she joked as she changed the pillowcases. "How about a clean shirt?"

"Are you going to help me change that, too?"

"Nah," she said, managing to keep her voice even. "I think you can handle that."

She grabbed a white T-shirt from his drawer. He pulled on the bottom of the shirt he was wearing and began tugging it up. Her eyes were immediately drawn to the smooth brown skin covering his six-pack abs. He blew out a breath and coughed. Unbelievably, he was having a hard time untangling himself from his shirt. The man who'd carried her with ease was losing a battle with a few ounces of cotton? Obviously, he was sicker than he let on. "Here, let me help."

Roz freed his head and arms, tossed the damp shirt on the floor, then helped him pull on the clean one.

"Thanks," he said, then flopped back onto the pillows as if sitting up was exhausting. "I hate being so weak. I don't understand how I got sick."

"I do," she said, pulling the blankets up to his chin, tucking him in like he was a child. But there was nothing childish about his body and nothing at all maternal about the feelings bubbling inside her. "You've been running yourself ragged for months. You've been taking care of me and the kids in addition to managing your company. You're only human. It was bound to catch up with you."

He shook his head. "I've always been busy. I own a string of gyms, so taking care of you guys is a piece of cake by comparison."

"Physically. But you're ignoring the emotional stress that comes with caring for three kids."

He closed his eyes in apparent agreement. Or maybe he was just too worn-out to argue. It didn't matter anyway. Regardless of how strong he was, he was sick and needed someone to take care of him.

The irony of the situation didn't escape her. He'd come to Sweet Briar to care for her and her children. Now she was on the road to recovery and he was flat on his back. She didn't wish him ill but she was glad for the opportunity to pay him back for all he'd done for her. It put balance into their previously unequal relationship. Before, she'd been the needy one. The taker. She'd had no choice but to lean on him.

Now he needed her. He'd learn how it felt to rely on someone else to provide his most basic needs. It wouldn't hurt to be the one with the power this time. So often, she'd chafed at having to rely on him for something as basic as getting in and out of the bathtub. She'd hated being so weak that she'd often needed assistance dressing herself. It had been empowering to help Paul change his undershirt just now. Not that she relished his weakness. She just gloried in her strength.

And it hadn't hurt to get a glimpse of his body. He'd seen hers enough times. While hers had become a bag of bones—thank goodness she'd put on a few pounds and was regaining some of the curves she'd lost—he was ripped. Clearly, he did more than own the gyms. He worked out there, as well. His abs were well-defined and his chest and shoulders were so muscular he could carry the weight of the world on them without breaking a sweat.

In a way, he'd done just that. He hadn't carried the actual planet. But her kids were her world and he'd taken care of them for months. He'd never once complained about the inconvenience or the disruption to his life. He'd just soldiered on, day after day, without taking a break. No wonder he was sick. Her shoulders slumped and her cheeks burned with shame. Paul was sick and she'd felt happy about being the strong one for a change.

Roz grabbed the balls of tissue from the side table and floor. She considered opening the window in order to let in fresh air, then decided against it. The nights had been pretty cool and she didn't want to make him worse. Taking one last look at him, she crossed the room and silently closed the door behind her. Paul might be leaving soon, but for the time being, he needed her. She would take care of him just as he'd taken care of her and her family.

And when the time came, she would let him go with a smile on her face. She owed him that much.

Chapter Thirteen

"Come in," Paul growled at the knock on the bedroom door. It had to be Roz since Nathaniel was playing in a basketball game and the girls had stayed after school to watch with Charlotte.

Rick had stopped by earlier and, despite Paul's protest, had examined him. After that unwanted checkup, Rick had diagnosed Paul with the flu, something Paul had already figured out. Rick had then given an unwelcome lecture about taking better care of himself and wasted more of Paul's time extolling the value of getting a flu shot.

At first, Paul had been glad to see his friend, believing Rick would convince Roz to stay away from him for the sake of her own health, but the good doctor hadn't agreed. Rick believed Roz was taking the necessary precautions to protect herself. He'd then pointed out that if the kids got sick after Paul left, Roz would have to take care of them. As if Paul didn't have enough to worry about. He'd spent the past hour brooding over that possibility.

"Aren't you Mr. Sunshine?" Roz asked, a smirk on her face. He'd forgotten how much she disliked whiners. So did he. But he just couldn't stop complaining.

"If you don't like my company, why do you keep bothering me?"

She laughed, a merry sound that, despite his aching body, stirred something inside him that was best left undisturbed. "I never said I didn't like your company, Mr. Grumpy. Besides, I come bearing gifts."

The aroma of chicken soup grew stronger as Roz came closer to the bed. The tray she was holding also contained a cup of tea and a small glass of orange juice. And was that Jell-O? He'd never been much of a fan, but now a bowl of that jiggling red stuff looked good. Oh, he must be sick.

Sitting up slowly, he leaned against the head of the bed, smoothed the blanket over his lap and reached for the tray. "Thanks. This looks good."

"You're welcome." Roz said. "I have ginger ale if you want some."

"Not now. Maybe later." He sampled the soup. It tasted too good to have come from a can. After taking a couple of swallows, he looked up at her. Dressed in an orange sweater and tight jeans that made his pulse race, she looked too good to spend the next hour sitting on metal bleachers. “Aren’t you going to Nathaniel’s game?”

“No. They play another game on Friday. I’ll go to that one. He understands that you’re sick.”

“I’m not so sick that I can’t manage on my own for a few hours. That’s what I would do if I was at home.” Of course, if Roz’s theory that he’d gotten run-down taking care of her and the kids was accurate, he wouldn’t be sick. Truth be told, Roz’s care disturbed him. It felt too right. Too natural. As if she were fulfilling a vow to care for him in sickness and in health, as he’d cared for her.

“Maybe. But you’re not alone at home. You’re here with me. I’m willing and able to nurse you back to health.”

“Still, it’s important to a kid to have his parents come to his sporting events.” Paul’s mother had attended as many games as she could. It had felt good knowing she was there even when he couldn’t see her. He’d always played better knowing she was watching, cheering him on.

“And I usually go. I missed some because I was sick, but other than that, I’ve been at every game. I attend all of the kids’ activities. I’ve been to every preschool graduation, kindergarten promotion and school musical. Nathaniel understands that you need someone to take care of you. Besides, Rick and Charlotte are taking the kids to the diner after the game. Nathaniel gets to hang out with Bobby and they all get to eat greasy food. Not to mention the added benefit of skipping vegetables because Charlotte won't make the kids eat them."

Charlotte had an aversion to vegetables and never let one past her lips. Not being a hypocrite, she wouldn't make the kids eat them either.

He swallowed some more soup, liking the way the liquid soothed his sore throat before making a warm path to his stomach. "You're a good mother."

Her eyes widened in surprise. What? It wasn't like he'd never complimented her. He closed his eyes. That's exactly what it was like. He'd never complimented her. Not that he hadn't thought she was a good mother. But saying the words out loud would have weakened the wall he was trying so hard to hold in place. It hadn't occurred to him that she might need a compliment, especially with Suzanne's struggles of late. He blew out a painful breath as he realized just how big a jerk he'd been. He'd been holding on to anger and resentment over her decision to marry Terrence. And though he'd recently let it go, he hadn't told Roz. As far as she knew, he still resented her. He owed her so many apologies.

"I'm sorry, Roz." He'd been so whiny and self-pitying.

"For what? Saying I'm a good mom? That's not an insult."

"I'm apologizing for not saying it sooner and for being such a jerk. You didn't deserve that." His voice caught in his throat, making it difficult to speak. He chalked it up to the flu—not to being overcome with emotion. At least, that was the story he told himself.

Her body stilled for a moment as his words sank in, then she dropped onto the mattress beside him. She was blinking rapidly, as if trying to hold back unwanted tears. One slid down her cheek and his gut clenched in agony. He'd done the unthinkable. He'd made Roz cry.

He lifted the tray and set it beside him, then, reaching out, wiped away the tear. Her skin was so soft, just as soft as the heart she hadn't been able to protect from the world. She'd always worn her heart on her sleeve, unable to hide her emotions no matter how hard she tried. Not that she really tried. She'd always been open to a fault.

"Sorry," she said, pulling away. "I don't know why I turned into a blubbering baby."

"I guess the stress of the past few months is taking its toll on you, too."

She shrugged. The doorbell rang and she stood as if eager to be away from him and this suddenly emotionally charged moment. "I'll be back for your tray later. Let me know if you need anything."

I need you. The words leaped to his mind and

nearly found a way out of his mouth. For the first time, that kind of thought didn't make him think he needed to have his head examined. Because he now knew that needing Roz didn't necessarily mean he would end up with a shredded heart.

Roz darted from the room, glad to have an excuse to get away from Paul and the emotions he aroused in her. For a moment, they'd been communicating, connecting in the way they had years ago. It had felt so right that she'd let down her guard and let him get a glimpse of what she'd been keeping inside. That had been a mistake.

They couldn't go back to what they'd had. They'd agreed the past was over and they were putting it behind them. That didn't mean just the anger. That meant everything. That included their hopes and dreams for a shared future. She needed to really accept that the love—or whatever it had been—was gone and wouldn't return. She'd wasted enough time wishing for the impossible. She'd been given a miracle: the gift of more time with her kids. Now she needed to get her life back on track.

She'd already talked to her boss about going back to work part-time in a few weeks. Maybe seeing Roz do that would help Suzanne overcome her fear. Maybe Suzanne needed to see that things were returning to normal. But Roz had more love in her heart to share. Love she wanted to give to a man.

Once her life was under control, she wanted to start dating again. This time she'd give her love to a man who wanted it and who would love her in return.

She reached the door just as the doorbell pealed again. Looked like they were anxious to see her. Or maybe someone needed to go to the bathroom.

"Hi, Mommy," Suzanne said as Roz swung open the door. "We had fun, but I missed you."

"I missed you, too." Roz hugged each of her children then looked at Nathaniel. "Well? How did it go?"

"We won. I scored twelve points and stole the ball once."

"Wow. That's great."

"Bobby scored fifteen."

Roz turned and smiled at her son's best friend and the best player on the team, according to Nathaniel. "Congratulations."

"Thanks." He grinned sheepishly.

"And thank you for taking them to the game," she said to Charlotte, who had come inside with the kids. "And for taking them to dinner. I really appreciate it."

Charlotte smiled. "No problem. It was nice to hang out with young women for a change."

"Do you mean us?" Megan asked, eyes wide.

"Yep."

Suzanne and Megan exchanged smiles and giggled. Megan tugged on Roz's hand. "Did you hear that, Mommy? We're young women."

"You are indeed. Two young women who need to take baths and then get ready for bed."

"Okay." They turned and raced to the stairs. When they reached the bottom, they turned. "Bye, Charlotte. Bye, Bobby."

"Bye," Charlotte replied, then looked at Roz. "They really are sweet."

"Thanks. How was Suzanne?"

Charlotte shrugged. "It's hard to tell. She didn't say too much about you. I don't know if that's good or bad. She did go on about a bad man throwing sand at people."

Roz sighed and told Charlotte about Paul's offhand comment. "I wonder if the school counselor is wrong. Maybe I need to consider the possibility that there are deeper issues I need to explore. Maybe she needs to see a psychologist."

"Give it another week or two. Bobby had a few issues, too. Different issues, but he worked them out in time. Suzanne could do the same." Charlotte gave her a hug. "I'm here if you need to talk."

"Thanks."

"Sure." Charlotte turned to Bobby, who was sitting next to Nathaniel on the couch. Bobby was whispering fiercely about something and Nathaniel's head bobbed. "Okay, guys. Bobby's dad is waiting in the car, so you'll have to finish this conversation tomorrow at school. And not during class time. At lunch. Got it?"

"Okay." Bobby jumped up and raced to the door. He started to follow Charlotte out, then paused and looked back at Nathaniel. "Remember what I told you. See you tomorrow."

Roz closed and locked the door, then turned to Nathaniel. "What was that all about?"

Nathaniel didn't meet her eyes. "Nothing."

"Okay," she said, deciding not to pry. Nathaniel was entitled to his secrets. She wrapped her arm around his shoulders. He was shooting up so fast, he would be taller than she was in no time. As it was, they were very nearly eye to eye. "So you had a good time?"

"Yeah. It would have been better if you were there."

"I'm sorry I wasn't."

"I know. You needed to take care of Uncle Paul like he used to take care of you."

"Right. You know if he wasn't sick he would have come, too."

"I know."

Roz sensed he wanted to say more, so she waited. When he didn't, she kissed his cheek. "Go on upstairs. I'll be up in a minute to say good-night."

He gave her a quick hug then bounded up the stairs.

Twenty minutes later, she was sitting between the girls, ready to read them a story.

"We should go into Uncle Paul's room so he can hear the story, too," Megan said, rising from her bed. "He likes reading about Little Red Riding Hood."

"I don't," Suzanne said. "I think the wolf is scary. I don't like when he pretends to be the grandmother so he can eat Little Red Riding Hood. Can we read something else?"

"Okay," Megan said, changing her selection without complaint. "How about 'Cinderella'? That's my favorite anyway."

"Mine, too. I like when the prince and Cinderella dance at the ball. They get married and live happily ever after."

"It sounds like you don't need me to read the story," Roz teased.

"Yes, we do. And we want to see the pictures. I like Cinderella's pretty dress. I wish I had a dress like that," Suzanne said, apparently no longer worried about the big bad wolf. Roz was going to have to purge their bookshelves. Not only to rid them of the nightmare-inducing fairy tales, but to make space for more empowering books. She didn't want her girls to grow up believing they needed a prince to rescue them. She wanted them to know they were responsible for solving their own problems and attaining their own happily-ever-after.

After she finished the story and tucked the girls

in for the night, she checked on Nathaniel, who was reading in bed. She gave him a tight hug and kissed his cheek. "Fifteen more minutes, then lights-out. And no reading under the covers with the flashlight."

He grinned. "I can't. I fell asleep with it on last night and the batteries died."

She laughed. "I'll get you some more."

She closed his door and told herself to go downstairs to her room, but her feet seemed to have a mind of their own. Telling herself she was just being thoughtful, she knocked on Paul's door. When he didn't answer, she turned the knob and stepped inside. The moonlight filtered through the open curtains, showing him in silhouette. Her breath caught in her throat as she watched him sleep. Unable to stop herself, she whispered the words she would never say to him if he were awake. "Oh, Paul, I wish we could have made it work. How I wish we could start over."

Then she slipped out the door, grateful that she'd finally given voice to the words that were hidden in her heart and even more grateful that he hadn't heard them.

Chapter Fourteen

I wish we could start over. Those words echoed in Paul's mind for the next three days. He wasn't sure if Roz had actually said them or if he'd imagined it. He'd had a fever after all, and Roz had starred in most of his dreams while he'd been sick. In every dream they'd been happy. Smiling. In love. Every morning when he awoke, his arms felt empty and his heart ached with loneliness that grew with each passing day. No matter how hard he tried, he couldn't shake it.

But those words didn't feel like part of a dream. They felt real, as if they'd actually been spoken. Or maybe it was just wishful thinking.

Roz wasn't acting any differently. She wasn't uncomfortable around him like he'd be if he'd bared his soul to her and silence had been the only response. If anything, she seemed happier, like a weight had been lifted from her slender shoulders. Maybe it was because of her improving health. Or maybe it was something else entirely.

Perhaps he should just ask her if she'd said it. Then he could stop tormenting himself. Of course, that could make things awkward between them. If he'd dreamed it, she might think he wanted a second chance with her. And if she had said it? What exactly would their future hold? He was still trying to figure out how he felt. Now that anger and resentment were no longer the dominant emotions he felt for her, he was struggling to name his feelings. But he couldn't make a wise decision while he was sick.

Not only that, they'd been dealing with so much these past few months. Given the tension and emotions, neither one of them was in a position to make a wise decision about something as serious as a relationship between them. So the best thing to do was to act like it had been a part of his dream. At least until things settled down.

Sitting up, he stretched and pushed all thoughts away. His fever had broken and he was starting to feel like himself. He was still a little weak, but his body no longer felt as if he'd been hit by a Mack truck. He took a quick shower and returned to his room. He needed to change the sheets and straighten the room.

As he pulled the soiled linen from the bed, his mind immediately went back to the night Roz had changed the sheets while he'd been lying in the bed. She'd been so near to him that her sweet scent had caressed him like gentle fingers, tempting him to take her into his arms. The only thing that had kept him from giving in to the urge to pull her down beside him was knowing he was contagious. He'd never knowingly put Roz's health at risk. Still, that hadn't kept him from watching her every move, getting a good view of her round bottom and her small, delectable breasts. He'd groaned aloud. When she'd looked at him, he'd played it off, pretending he'd groaned because of flu pain. His head and throat had ached with the flu that night, but another part of him had ached with desire.

He forced the memory from his mind. Hadn't he just decided that they needed time to figure out what they were going to do? Over the past dozen years, he'd built up an image of who Roz was in his mind and it wasn't pretty. He'd believed she was fickle and selfish and hundreds of other things just as awful.

And he'd been wrong. Roz was nothing like he'd pictured. At first he attributed the difference to the illness and her need for his help. If she was kind, it was because she was desperate and afraid to offend him. But with each day, she was getting stronger, more capable of taking care of herself and her kids, yet her personality hadn't changed for the worse. Quite the opposite. Her sense of humor and spirit of adventure were gradually returning, making her a joy to be around. She was becoming the same girl he'd fallen in love with all those years ago.

No, that wasn't right. Sure, Roz still possessed many of the same traits she'd had as a teenager. She still had a dry wit. She still rolled her eyes when she found something ridiculous and chewed on her bottom lip when she disagreed with someone but was trying to avoid an argument.

But she had a strength now that she'd lacked at seventeen. A confidence that everything would be okay because she was going to make it okay. He knew that if he hadn't come to her aid, she would have found a way to care for her kids. Although he liked thinking of himself as the hero, he knew she was no damsel in distress. Her strength made her even more desirable.

He added his T-shirt and pajama bottoms to the pile of sheets, deciding to wash them, as well. He didn't want his germy laundry mixing with Roz's. The rational part of him knew germs weren't passed that way, but he didn't see any harm in being cautious. Roz's health was too important for him to risk. She was too important.

He was buttoning his shirt when his door burst open, banging against the wall and sending a picture crashing to the floor. Suzanne burst into his room. "Guess what, Uncle Paul?"

"What?"

"My tooth just came out!" She held out her hand as she ran across the room to give him a closer look. Sure enough, there was a tiny tooth in the middle of her palm.

"That's great."

Plopping onto the bed, she opened her mouth and pointed to a small hole between two teeth. "I was wiggling it with my tongue and it just popped out. Now I'm a big girl like Megan."

"That you are."

"I'm going to put it under my pillow so the tooth fairy can bring me a dollar." She was positively beaming with glee. He hadn't seen her this happy in a long time and the sight warmed his heart.

"That's a good idea. Did you show your mom?"

"I'm about to."

"About to what?" Roz asked, coming into the room.

"Look," Suzanne exclaimed. She hopped from the bed and scampered to stand before her mother. She opened her mouth and held out her hand to show Roz her missing tooth.

"That's wonderful." Roz stooped down and gave her daughter a big hug. "I knew that tooth would come out soon."

"I'm big."

"You most certainly are. Now go put that tooth under your pillow."

Paul watched the interaction between mother and child. Roz might not have had loving parents growing up, but she was the best mother he knew. Besides his own mother, that was. Despite Terrence's death and her illness, Roz had kept her little family together. Would she look for another man to complete that family unit?

The thought of Roz falling in love and marrying someone else stopped his heart. He wanted her to be happy, of course, but the idea of her finding that happiness with someone else was unsettling. Which just went to show how selfish he was. He couldn't figure out if he wanted her, but he was certain he didn't want her with another man. But if he decided things wouldn't work out between them, he had to face the fact that some lucky guy would come into her life and give her the love she deserved.

"Sorry about that," Roz said. She bent over and picked up the picture, and he found his eyes drawn to her firm backside. She inspected the picture for damage before hanging it back on the wall.

"About what?" He was so distracted that he had lost track of the conversation.

"Suzanne busting in on you. I've told the kids over and over not to disturb you, but I guess she forgot. Losing that first tooth is a big deal."

Suzanne hadn't disturbed him. But Roz was definitely messing with him. Dressed in a fitted pair of jeans that hugged her sweet bottom and a long-sleeved shirt just tight enough to hint at her slim curves, she looked like a dream. His dream. "It's no problem. Besides, I feel much better. I was about to toss these things into the washing machine."

Her eyes moved from his face to his chest and widened as if she was just noticing his shirt was open to the waist. She froze and he found himself unable to move either. The air between them fairly crackled with sexual tension. Time stood still and he couldn't breathe. Her chest rose and then fell as she blew out a breath. She blinked and looked somewhere over his shoulder.

"I can do that for you," she said, reaching for the sheets. Okay, so she was going to pretend the air between them hadn't been hot enough to scorch them both. He was good with that. It was probably for the best. They didn't need the complication. He fastened the buttons, leaving only the top one undone.

"No. I'll take care of it. You've done enough for me."

She laughed. "You have it backward. I can never do enough to repay you for everything you've done for me and my kids. If I haven't said it before, I'll say it now. I really am grateful, Paul. More grateful than you will ever know."

"You're welcome." The words came out easily because he really meant them. Yet a part of him wanted more than her gratitude. He needed to think about what that something more was. He'd made a mistake once of not knowing how deep his feelings for her were. He wasn't going to repeat it.

Roz stepped outside Paul's bedroom and leaned against the wall. Closing her eyes, she breathed deeply and tried to calm herself. Her heart continued to pound in her chest. My goodness, that man looked good. Paul had always been handsome, but he had become even better looking with age. The teenage body she'd always admired had developed into the fit body of a man. His chest had filled out and his shoulders, arms and back had developed, as well. He was easily the best-built man in North Carolina. Heck, in North America.

Why was she acting this way? She'd seen his chest before. Just days ago, she'd helped him change his shirt and the sight hadn't made her break into a sweat. But then he'd been so ill and she'd been preoccupied with his health. It had been easier to stifle her reaction. She definitely wasn't immune to him now.

She blew out a breath and opened her eyes. Paul stood a foot away from her. He was staring at her, an unreadable expression on his face. Words fled and she couldn't think of a plausible explanation as to why she was loitering outside his door. She tried to smile but her lips only trembled.

Moving slowly, as if in a fog, he closed the distance between them until they were mere inches apart. The sheets clasped in his large hands formed the only barrier between them. The cotton fabric brushed against her breasts. The sheets were thin and didn't block the heat surging from his body, wrapping around her and singeing her skin. She knew her heart would go up in flames if she didn't back away, but she didn't have the strength to move.

He reached out and touched her face. His fingers were gentle, yet they left a trail of fire behind them. Her brain said to move away, to protect her heart, but her body shot down that notion immediately. His touch felt so good. She wasn't going anywhere. He dragged his finger across her mouth and a moan slipped through her lips. His eyes were riveted on hers and they communicated wordlessly. Perfectly.

They'd been in this position once before and they'd been interrupted before she'd been satisfied. Roz wasn't going to let that happen again. Reaching out, she put her hands on either side of Paul's face, caressing his skin. He hadn't shaved over the past few days, and his normally clean-shaven jaw was now covered with a short beard. The hair felt good to the touch and her fingers delighted at the feel. Standing on her tiptoes, she brushed her lips against his.

Heaven. That was the only word to describe it. Her lips tingled and those tingles shot through every inch of her body, racing from the top of her head to the tips of her toes. She felt him inhale, then freeze, and the fear that he would pull away stopped her heart. Before she could react or even breathe, his arms wrapped around her waist and he stepped closer to her, pressing their bodies together. She'd been in heaven before, but there wasn't a word to describe what she felt now. Every nerve ending in her body short-circuited with pleasure and her entire body weakened until she thought she might dissolve into a puddle of desire.

She could have kissed Paul forever. She felt him pull away and protested, stepping closer to him. He chuckled and stepped back. "The kids are coming."

The haze in her mind was slow to clear. Too slow.

"Why are you kissing?" Megan asked.

"Oh, goody. Mommy and Uncle Paul are kissing. And I didn't have to make them this time." Suzanne clapped her hands. "Mommy and Uncle Paul are getting married, just like Cinderella and Prince Charming."

Chapter Fifteen

Paul looked at the girls' smiling faces and then at Roz's strained one. He searched for the right words to set the girls straight without hurting any of their feelings. He was still trying to figure out what he felt for Roz. One thing he knew for sure, neither he nor Roz was in the position to make a permanent commitment to each other. But the girls looked so thrilled at the prospect that he knew they were going to be very disappointed to hear that a marriage wasn't in the offing.

He could let Roz be the one to let them down, but that would be unfair to her. He didn't know how the girls would react, but if there were any negative feelings, he would rather they be directed at him and not Roz. That way Roz's relationship with her daughters wouldn't be affected.

"We aren't getting married," he said.

"But you were kissing," Megan said. "We saw you."

"That's true. But not everybody who kisses gets married," he said. Paul kept his gaze on the kids although he really wanted to see how Roz was reacting to his words. Though he'd taken the lead, it wouldn't hurt for her to chime in now and say something.

"But Snow White and the prince got married," Suzanne said.

"And Tiana and Prince Naveen, too," Megan added.

"And Belle and the prince who used to be the beast," Suzanne said.

"I know all the stories," Paul said as he realized they were going to list each and every Disney princess, like young lawyers laying out evidence to prove their point. "But those aren't real people."

The girls looked scandalized so he rushed to continue. "And your mom and I are real people. It doesn't mean we don't care for each other. It just means we aren't in love with each other and don't want to get married."

"You don't love Mommy?" Suzanne said, sounding positively crushed.

"You shouldn't kiss people if you don't love them," Megan said. "That's not nice."

"Listen," Roz said, interrupting before the girls could flay his heart any further, "Uncle Paul is right. We aren't going to get married. But he is still your uncle and still my friend. So how about we go outside and play on the swing for a while."

"Okay, Mommy," Suzanne said, grabbing her mother's hand and sticking out her tongue at him over her shoulder before descending the stairs. Megan wagged a disapproving finger in Paul's face and then followed Roz and Suzanne. Who would have known the girls' disappointment and disgust with him would hurt so much?

And what about Roz? She hadn't looked at him directly once. Perhaps she was embarrassed about initiating the kiss? She shouldn't be. She may have made the first move, but if the truth be told, she'd only beaten him by a second. He'd been a breath away from pulling her into his arms. But even so, he knew that was a reaction to the desire that had been building between them. They needed time and space to rationally figure out what would be the best thing for them to do. He just hoped Roz knew that, too.

He picked up the laundry from where he'd dropped it and headed toward the basement laundry room. Once the washer was loaded and going, he went upstairs. Roz and the girls were in the yard, so he decided to make breakfast for them. He told himself he wasn't exactly trying to bribe them, but he wanted to get back into their good graces.

He set the table while cooking waffles, frying bacon and scrambling eggs. When it was all done, he called everyone in to eat. Nathaniel piled his plate high with food, pleased with the elaborate meal. It took the girls a while, but eventually they set their disappointment aside and began talking to him again. Apparently, while they were outside playing, Roz had convinced Megan and Suzanne that being friends with him was good enough for her.

Not that he'd decided that friendship was all he wanted. He hadn't. What he'd decided was that he didn't want to make another mistake with her. But since the girls were too young to understand the difference, he didn't try and explain it. Heck, he barely understood it himself.

After breakfast was done, Nathaniel put his dishes into the sink, then ran out of the kitchen. A minute later, he was back, a piece of paper in his hand. He gave it to Roz, then smiled tentatively at her. What was that about? Her normally gregarious son appeared timid. Apprehension filled her as he handed a similar paper to Paul, who looked at her with a question in his eyes.

She opened the folded piece of orange paper and then read it. It was a flyer for Sweet Briar's harvest festival, which would be held two weekends from now. She knew about the festival, although she had no idea of the specific events and when they would be held. She and Paul had already talked about taking the kids there.

She skimmed the flyer. The carnival, parade, walk/run and an auction to raise funds for the youth center all sounded promising. She continued to read. There was going to be a talent show and a—what? A ball? She hadn't heard about that. No wonder Nathaniel looked so sheepish. He was at an age where he wasn't sure just how he felt about girls.

"We got this at the youth center yesterday and I forgot to give it to you. Can we go?" Nathaniel asked.

"Sure. To some things. It would be a bit exhausting to try and do everything. We can sit down as a family and decide what to do, okay?" Roz glanced at Paul, who nodded his agreement.

"What are we deciding?" Megan asked.

"About the harvest festival weekend," Nathaniel said before either adult could answer.

"Oh. Are we going? Miss Joni told us all about it," Megan asked, clapping her hands. "I want to be in the parade. They said we can decorate our bikes. They're going to give us candy to throw to the people. I'm going to eat mine. And I want to go to the carnival. They have games and cotton candy."

"I want to be in the race," Nathaniel added. "I'm the fastest kid in my class."

"That sounds good," Roz said.

"We don't have to go to the ball if that will make you tired," Nathaniel said.

"There's a ball?" Suzanne exclaimed. "I want to go. I want to wear a princess dress just like Tiana and Cinderella. And I want to dance with a prince."

Roz kept herself from frowning at that last part. Her little girl was actually enthusiastic about something for the first time in a long while. But why did it have to be the ball? That was the activity Roz was hoping to skip. She didn't even have a plausible excuse such as the lack of a babysitter, because the Sweet Briar ball was open to everyone, including kids. According to the flyer, there would be a chaperoned party room for the children, separate from the adults, but there would be daddy and daughter dances as well as mother and son dances.

Roz looked at the glow on Suzanne's face and knew she wouldn't sit this event out. "That sounds like fun."

"I want a pink princess dress with lots of sparkles. And I want shiny red shoes with bows."

"I want a blue dress," Megan said. "And I want blue shoes. Or black. I want them shiny, too. With high heels."

"And I want to carry some flowers," Suzanne chimed in, warming up to the whole idea.

"I don't know about carrying flowers," Roz said, trying to slow them down before they got carried away, "but we can get you a flower to wear on your dress."

"And I want a crown with diamonds in it. Just like Tiana," Suzanne added.

"I'm not sure we can do diamonds, but maybe we can find something like them. Or maybe we can make a crown out of flowers."

As the girls continued to chatter about what they wanted to wear, Roz sneaked a peek at Paul, who was watching the entire conversation, an amused expression on his handsome face. She hoped he didn't think she was expecting him to go with her. Goodness no. She was perfectly fine going on her own. She'd set him straight on that later.

"What do you want to wear, Nathaniel?" Paul asked when the girls took a breath from talking about getting their fingernails polished.

Nathaniel's mouth dropped open. "Are you kidding?"

Paul laughed. "Yes, I am."

"Good. Bobby told me he has to go to the ball because of Charlotte. She thought of the dance and she has to go because it's her job. I'll go if you want, but I'm not going to dance with any girls or anything."

"You aren't going to dance with me?" Suzanne asked, looking crushed. "Don't you love me?"

"Of course I love you. You're my sister. I'll dance with you and Megan. I just meant I'm not going to dance with any other girls. Well, besides Mom that is."

"Thank you," Roz said.

"And, Uncle Paul, you're going to dance with Mommy, right?" Suzanne asked.

Roz's mouth went dry even as her palms became sweaty. Every eye in the room focused on Paul, including Roz's. Roz had spent a good thirty minutes explaining to Megan and Suzanne that she and Paul weren't in love and that they weren't getting married. She thought she'd been successful. Apparently she hadn't.

She understood their difficulty. The kiss she and Paul shared had had her fantasizing about a future together. His words had doused the flame of hope flickering inside her. Though he'd been speaking to the girls, she'd received the message loud and clear. He might have given in to the desire simmering between them, but he didn't want her. Message received.

"Of course I'm going to dance with your mom," Paul said, picking up Suzanne and setting her on his lap. "I'm going to dance with all three of you. You'll be the prettiest girls there."

"But Mommy will be the most prettiest, right, Uncle Paul?" Suzanne prodded. What she lacked in tact, she definitely made up for in determination. And apparently she was determined to match the adults in her life.

Paul winked at Roz and her heart skipped a beat. Darn. Where was her brain? The man had been clear. "Absolutely. Your mom is the prettiest girl I know."

"Mom is the prettiest girl in the whole wide world," Suzanne said.

"Oh, stop, you two."

"It's true," Suzanne said. "You're pretty again now that you have hair. You were ball-headed before and really scary looking. Now you look like pretty Mommy again."

Roz tried to ignore the pain that stabbed her in the heart. She knew it was ridiculous to worry about something as trivial as her appearance in general and her hair specifically, but still she ached at her daughter's innocent words.

One of the stylists at Fit To Be Dyed hair salon had mentioned the availability of wigs for cancer patients. When Roz's hair had begun to fall out in patches, another had suggested hair extensions. Roz had turned them both down. Then, last week, she'd gone out and bought a wig. She felt better, but the change in Suzanne had been nothing short of astounding. Though Suzanne knew Roz was wearing a wig, her shoulder-length hair symbolized healing and health. Suzanne was no longer forced to face her mother's illness every time she looked at her. The wig had taken away Suzanne's fear.

Suzanne smiled at Roz, unaware that she'd hurt her mother's feelings. From the sympathy on his face, it was clear that Paul knew. But she didn't want his pity. She didn't want anyone's pity.

"Hey, guys," Paul said, filling the silence that now hung over the room. "I have an idea. It's such a nice day. Why don't we do something outside?"

"Like what?" Megan asked. "We already played on the swings."

"Whatever you choose."

"Can we go on the boat again?" Nathaniel asked.

"It's best to get our tickets in advance for that."

"I know. Can we go to the zoo?" Megan asked. "My class went on a field trip there last year and it was so much fun. I liked looking at the animals."

"Yeah. Let's go to the zoo," Suzanne said.

"If that's what you want." Paul looked at Roz. "Where is the zoo?"

"Charlotte."

"I'm okay with that if you are."

Roz nodded. "That's fine with me."

The three children cheered loudly. Roz was glad about the change of subject. And she had to admit a day outside in the fresh air did sound heavenly. The spontaneous trip was just what she needed to get her mind off the kiss she and Paul had shared.

The kids raced from the room. Roz started to follow when Paul grabbed her hand, stopping her in her tracks. He turned her gently until they were facing each other. Reaching out, he ran a hand over her hair as he stared into her eyes. “You’re still beautiful, Roz. Just as beautiful as you’ve ever been.”

Her eyes filled with tears. One trickled down her cheek and he brushed it away. “Sorry,” she murmured.

“You don’t have to be sorry. You don’t need to hide how you feel from me.”

Of course she did. He was the one person in the world she could never let see her feelings. She couldn’t let him know that she’d fallen in love with him again and that she loved him with all her heart. Not after he’d just made it clear they didn’t have a future together.

“Here we go,” Paul said as he set the tray of hot dogs and bags of chips on the table. Nathaniel and Megan followed with the drinks they’d insisted they could carry.

“Thanks,” Roz said. She grabbed the packets of mustard, ketchup and relish and began to open them so the kids could squirt the condiments of their choice on their hot dogs.

“This is the most fun,” Megan said after she sat down.

“I agree,” Paul said. And he was having a great time. He hadn’t been to the zoo since his fifth grade field trip.

He slid into the chair next to Roz. She glanced up at him, a startled expression on her face. What was that about? Did it bother her to have him sit beside her? He couldn't imagine why it would. They'd been enjoying the day. She'd laughed more than she had in weeks. But, come to think of it, she did seem to shift away from him whenever he came around. Perhaps she wanted to reestablish the distance between them. But why? She was the one who'd kissed him, not that he was complaining. Maybe this was her way of insuring they didn't cross that boundary again.

Roz was animated as she chatted with the kids while they ate. Her eyes danced in her face and she giggled like a young girl. He joined in occasionally, but mostly he just watched.

He hadn't been lying this morning when he'd told her she was just as beautiful as she'd ever been. Her eyes were just as bright and her skin had a healthy glow. And she was starting to put on a little weight, which he found incredibly sexy. True, her glorious hair was gone, but that didn't make her any less appealing. He'd liked her without hair. Not every woman could pull it off. But then not every woman possessed Roz's cheekbones and stunning face.

He also understood her decision to wear a wig. Doing so had made a difference in Suzanne's attitude. Besides, her beauty was more than external. It shone from within. It was the way she loved her children. The concern she showed for her friends. The consideration she showed everyone she encountered. It was in the grace she demonstrated as she faced a challenge that could have shattered her. But Roz had not broken. She'd faced cancer with strength and courage. Not once during all of her many visits to the hospital had he witnessed her being unkind to anyone. She'd withstood the pain and illness that accompanied her chemotherapy and surgery and maintained her sweet personality.

He admired Roz. More than that, he liked her. If he wasn't careful, he would fall in love with her again. He wanted to be sure it was right for them before he walked down that road. Roz was the one woman who had the power to bring him to his knees. If things didn't work out, he wouldn't be able to rise again. Loving her was risky. Now he had to decide whether it was a risk he was willing to take.

At least he was officially free to take it. Last week, Kristin had finally returned one of his calls. She'd confirmed that they were well and truly over and quite bluntly told him to leave her alone. She was involved with a fellow surgeon and didn't want an ex-boyfriend who couldn't get the message hanging around.

He noticed that the table had grown silent and looked up. Four sets of eyes were staring at him. "What?"

The kids laughed uproariously.

"What?" he asked again.

"You were just sitting there, frozen, with a chip halfway to your mouth," Roz said. She smiled and his heart lurched, startling him with its power as it all but jumped out of his chest.

He looked down at his hand. Sure enough, it was hovering several inches away from his mouth. Luckily, his mouth wasn't gaping open or a fly might have flown in. Wouldn't that have been a sight to see? He dropped the chip back into the bag. "You caught me. My mind wandered away from me."

Suzanne frowned and looked around. "Where did it go? I didn't see anything. And how did it get out? Did it crawl out your ears?"

He laughed. "That's just an expression. It means I was thinking of something else."

"What?" she asked.

There was no time like the present. He needed to get Suzanne used to him being gone. Even if he and Roz decided to pursue their relationship, he still had a business to run. For the time being, that required being on the road. "I was thinking that I need to go back to Florida."

The smile slid from Roz's face as she withdrew into herself. The light that had been animating her expression faded. She didn't say a word, just as he knew she wouldn't. He wasn't the only one who'd put up walls between them. Roz had done her fair share of erecting barriers, as well.

"But why, Uncle Paul?" Megan asked.

"Don't you love us anymore?" Suzanne asked, setting the last bite of her hot dog onto the foil wrapper. All of her previous joy seeped from her like air from a balloon.

"Girls, we knew Uncle Paul wasn't going to stay forever. He only came to help while I was sick. I'm not sick anymore, so he can go back to his home. Now, let's finish eating and walk around a little bit longer before it's time to leave." Roz's voice was filled with forced cheer. She'd plastered on a smile so fake it could have been made of wax. He wondered if the kids noticed.

"I'll be back," he said firmly. "Remember, I promised to take you to the ball."

The girls nodded glumly and he felt like a heel. But they knew he would leave at some point. And he would come back. That was a promise he intended to keep.

They gathered the trash, trudged to the garbage can and then shoved it in. That done, Roz hustled the girls to the ladies' restroom while he and Nathaniel went to the men's room. Before they stepped inside, Nathaniel pulled on his arm, stopping him. Paul looked into his nephew's face. He looked as serious as an eleven-year-old kid could manage.

"You don't have to tell the girls you're coming back if you aren't. I know you have to go back to Florida. I'll take my sisters to the dance. And don't worry about Mom. Bobby and I have a plan."

That sounded ominous. "What kind of plan?"

"We're going to find her a boyfriend. Bobby said

his dad used to be sad because he didn't have a girlfriend. Now his dad is happy because he's going to marry Charlotte. Bobby's happy, too, because Charlotte's going to be his mom. He already calls her mom sometimes since she said it's okay."

Nathaniel looked up at him and Paul managed to smile even though the idea of Roz getting a boyfriend still knocked him for a loop.

"Miss Joni's brother is going to be at the ball. He's in the army so he's strong and brave. He came to the youth center a couple of times and I liked him. I'm going to ask him to dance with Mom. She's pretty and nice, so we think they'll fall in love and get married. Then she'll have a husband again and we'll have a stepdad."

Paul found it hard to breathe. "Miss Joni's brother, huh?"

"Yeah. What do you think?"

He thought he wanted to be talking about anything but this. He'd seen the other man around and found him impressive. "How do you know he doesn't already have a girlfriend?"

"Bobby told me he heard Miss Joni tell Charlotte she wants to introduce him to her friends. She wouldn't have said that if he already had a girlfriend."

"Maybe not. But maybe your mother won't like being set up."

"She won't mind," Nathaniel said confidently. "She wants to get married again."

"How do you know this?" Why was he taking the word of a kid? Especially one with questionable sources.

Nathaniel rolled his eyes. "All girls want to get married. That's why they read fairy tales. So they can learn how to get a husband and live happily ever after."

Paul blew out a relieved breath. Nathaniel didn't have proof.

"Plus, I heard her tell Charlotte that she was ready to date again."

"Really?" The relief faded.

"Yeah. They know someone who helps people find husbands. I forgot what it is called."

"Matchmaker?"

"Yeah. A matchmaker. They were laughing and Mom said she was going to call her and see if she could find her a boyfriend. Now she won't have to. Bobby and I already have one picked out for her." Nathaniel looked so pleased that Paul could only stare at him. Apparently, Nathaniel thought the conversation was over, because he stepped around Paul and into the restroom. Paul followed on legs that could have weighed a thousand pounds.

Roz was ready to date again. He shouldn't be surprised. She was still a young woman, one with a new lease on life. No doubt she wanted to experience all life had to offer. Truthfully, he hadn't expected her to remain in limbo forever. What was unexpected was the hollow feeling in his gut. It was as if each of Nathaniel's words were a fist pummeling him until he wanted to curl up into a ball and cry.

Well, that wouldn't do. He couldn't stand here in limbo either. He followed Nathaniel into the men's room, all the while making plans. It was more imperative than ever that he take the time to straighten out his feelings. And then, if his feelings were real, as he suspected they were, he'd have to figure out a plan of action. He'd lost Roz once because he failed to act. He wasn't going to make that same mistake again. Not in this life.

Chapter Sixteen

Roz pulled the cookie sheet out of the oven and placed it on the stove. Moving by rote, she removed each of the chocolate chip cookies with a spatula and placed them on a cooling rack. The aroma made her nostalgic for the carefree days of childhood, which was ridiculous. Her aunt had never baked cookies or anything else for her. No one had.

It was late and everyone else was sleeping. She knew she should be asleep, too, but she was too restless to do anything other than toss and turn for hours, which was the last thing she wanted to do. Rather, it was next to last. The last thing she wanted to do was say goodbye to Paul. He was leaving first thing in the morning. Apparently, he couldn't wait to shake the dust of this small town from his feet. And wasn't she being catty and petty for being disgruntled?

As she'd told the kids, she'd always known Paul was going to leave. And since she was doing so much better, there was no need for him to stay. What happened to her promise to say goodbye with a smile?

Roz scooped up the last cookie with a little more pressure than was required, causing the cookie sheet to slide off the stove. Without thinking, she grabbed it, forgetting that it had just come from a hot oven. She cried out and let go of the pan and it clattered to the floor. Hurrying to the sink, she ran her hand under the cold water as tears streamed down her face. She wasn't sure if she was crying because of the pain in her hand or the pain in her heart.

"What's wrong?"

She jumped at Paul's voice. She shouldn't be surprised that he came at her sound of distress. That's who he was. Ready and able to help her at the slightest hint of trouble. But he was leaving in a few hours and she needed to get used to standing on her own two feet again.

"Nothing. I just burned my hand." She spoke over her shoulder.

He crossed the room, took her hand into his and looked at it. "How?"

"I wasn't thinking. The cookie sheet slipped and

I grabbed it. It's not a big deal. I've burned myself before."

She pulled her hand free, then dabbed at the moisture with a paper towel.

"I'll get the ointment."

She didn't bother to argue. Paul was going to do what Paul was going to do.

"What are you doing up at this hour?" he asked when he returned.

"I couldn't sleep, so I decided to bake."

"I see." He opened the tube, then held out his hand. She tried to steel herself for the electricity that always shot through her when they touched, but it was a waste of time. Her body reacted as strongly as ever. Why wouldn't it stop? She needed to become immune to him in order to become attracted to someone else. A man whose heart was available and who would welcome her love. One with whom she didn't share a complicated past. That wouldn't happen if she couldn't get over Paul.

His fingers were gentle as he smoothed the ointment onto the burn. The pain began to subside. He finished rubbing in the medicine, but he continued to hold her hand. She knew she should remove her hand from his, but she didn't have the strength. Besides, he was leaving in the morning, so what could it hurt to enjoy this one moment of time?

The night was so quiet she could hear her heartbeat. She hadn't turned on the television or one of her playlists, because she didn't want to disturb anyone. The silence became a blanket that wrapped around the two of them, cocooning them in warm intimacy.

"I'm coming back, you know," Paul said. His deep voice was soft, yet the power of its conviction made her tremble.

"You don't need to do that," she said, ignoring her deepest longing for him to return. She couldn't imagine not seeing him every day. She'd grown accustomed to his presence and enjoyed the rare, quiet moments they shared. "You've put your life on hold much too long. I'm better and can handle it from here."

"You don't want me to come back?"

He sounded hurt and disappointed. But why? He should be relieved he was no longer obliged to take care of her. Now he could return to the life he'd left behind without guilt.

"You've done so much already. Way above and beyond the call of duty. But it's time to get on with your life. And the kids and I need to get on with ours."

"And Suzanne?"

"She's so much better now. Surely you've noticed. She's not worried about me dying. And since things are no longer tense between you and me, she's been able to relax. Her teacher said that she plays with the other kids and answers questions in class. And she's stopped sucking her thumb. She's becoming more like her old self."

He dropped her hand. "So you don't need me anymore."

She'd always need him. Always want him. But she couldn't say that. She couldn't tie him to her indefinitely. And as noble as Paul was, he'd stay if she asked. But she couldn't hold on to him that way. She wanted him to stay because he wanted to be with her and for no other reason. He deserved to spend his life with the woman of his choosing. He deserved to be free. But she couldn't say all that without breaking down. "I think I can take it from here."

He nodded. "What about the ball? I promised the girls I would dance with them."

He'd promised her, as well. "I'll think of something. I'm sure Rick will dance with them."

"And Joni's brother."

"Brandon?"

"No. The other one. The soldier."

She raised her eyebrows at his sharp tone. "Russell? I suppose if I ask him he will. The girls don't know him very well, though." And how odd was it that Paul would mention Joni's brother now. Perhaps he was trying to convince her that she had other relationship options so she wouldn't hang her hopes on him. She'd already received that message loud and clear. She didn't need him to play matchmaker in order to drive home his point. "Anyway, we'll be fine."

"Okay. I'll see you in the morning." He turned and walked from the room.

Roz went back to the stove, unable to watch him walk away from her again. She knew if she wasn't careful, she'd beg him to stay.

"I wish you weren't leaving, Uncle Paul," Suzanne said, giving him a big hug. She held on longer than either Nathaniel or Megan had. He felt wetness on his neck and eased her back slightly. "I love you a lot and I'm going to miss you."

"Don't cry, Suzanne." He wiped tears from her face. "I love you a lot, too."

Her bottom lip trembled and his heart broke just a little bit more. "Then why don't you stay?"

"I can't. I'm going to tell you a secret. But you can't tell anyone else, okay?"

She nodded, then twisted her fingers over her lips and wiped an arm over her face. Her eyes sparkled and she perked up at the thought of knowing something her older siblings didn't.

He leaned closer. The wind blew and a few leaves drifted from the large tree in the backyard. Even though the kids had a swing set, they preferred the tire swing he'd hung from a thick branch. Megan was swinging there now and singing a song she'd made up. The words didn't rhyme and the melody was inconsistent, but her voice was clear and filled with joy. Nathaniel was tossing a football into the air and catching it against his chest.

"What's your secret, Uncle Paul?"

"I'm coming back. I promised to take you to the dance and I'm going to do that."

"Are you going to dance with me?"

"Yes."

"And Mommy?"

He smiled. "Yes. I'm going to dance with your mommy. But remember, this is our secret."

Suzanne giggled. "Okay. I won't tell anyone. Even Mommy."

He met Suzanne's eyes, happy to see a twinkle there. Her joy touched his heart. He didn't hold out much hope that she would keep the secret. It would probably leak out before the day was over. But that didn't matter since it really wasn't a secret. He'd told them he was going to escort them to the ball. What mattered was that Suzanne knew he would be returning. That he would always keep his promises to her. "That's good. Otherwise, it won't be a secret."

He hugged her one last time. Before he stood, he whispered in her ear. "I'm going to bring you a present when I come back."

"What is it?"

He chuckled at her breathless anticipation. "I'm not going to tell you. But you'll like it."

He waved to the other children, then watched as Suzanne raced over to the swing before he went into the kitchen. Roz was staring out the window. She turned to face him, her arms crossed over her breasts. He took her all in, wanting to memorize everything about her so he could carry that image with him. Dressed in a long-sleeved green-and-gray-striped shirt and a gray denim skirt, she looked both casual and sexy. She'd always been beautiful, but these past few weeks she'd become practically irresistible.

It was good that he was leaving for a while. If he stayed much longer, he'd put the moves on her. It was better that he sort out his feelings before taking any action. He didn't want to approach her unless he was 100 percent sure of the direction he wanted to take.

"So, you're ready to go?" Her voice quivered a bit. She didn't look directly at him, but rather stared at some point just over his shoulder.

"Yes. I'll call you when I get there."

"You don't have to do that." It was as if she was trying to end things right now by building a solid wall between them.

Or maybe it was something else entirely. When he'd left her to go to college, he'd promised to call her the minute he arrived at school. That first day had been more hectic than he'd thought it would be and he hadn't found time to call her until the following morning. He'd tried to explain that the school administration had arranged events from the moment he stepped on campus until late that night. He'd had to get his room organized, and then hustle from one end of the campus to the other to participate in everything from cookouts to a workshop on campus life. And the promised contact had only diminished from there. He hadn't realized it then, but he knew now just how badly he'd let her down. No wonder she didn't trust him.

This was different, even if she didn't believe it. For one thing, he wasn't an eighteen-year-old embarking on an exciting adventure. He was a grown man going home to take care of business and sort through his feelings. Then he was coming back here to see what was going on between him and Roz. There was no going back, of course. There never was. And he didn't want to go back. He was starting to believe that they could put the past behind them and move forward. Together.

What would a future look like for the two of them? It would definitely be different from the one they had planned years ago. They had three children to think about, for one thing. He loved those children with his whole heart. He couldn't love them more if they were his own kids. There was no way he would do anything to hurt them. If he and Roz got together it was going to be for the long haul. There would be no going back and forth. The kids deserved certainty in their lives.

There was a time when he didn't believe he could ever forgive Roz for what he saw as her betrayal. Now he realized they both were responsible for the demise of their relationship. They'd been too young to make such a commitment to each other. But they were older now, and, hopefully, wiser.

He closed the distance between them and gave her a gentle hug, then kissed her cheek. "I'll call you when I get there."

She nodded and he quickly walked through the house and out the front door, not slowing until he'd gotten into the car and driven down the block. His chest ached as he drove farther away. He missed them already. He was more certain than ever that he would return to them for more than the ball. He would be back for good.

Roz took a deep breath and steeled her spine as she watched Paul drive away. Being sad was ridiculous. She'd always known he wouldn't stay forever. She just didn't think it would hurt this badly to watch him leave. And he wouldn't be back, no matter what he said. This goodbye was final.

And it should be. There was no reason for him to return. He'd cared for her children when she hadn't been able to just as he'd promised. It wasn't his fault that she'd fallen in love with him again. She was responsible for controlling her emotions—not him.

And with that admission Roz ended all dreams of sharing her life with Paul. It was time to put that dream to bed and look to the future. Hopefully, it included love and romance.

The back door slammed and her kids trekked into the house.

"What are we going to do today?" Megan asked. It was a teacher institute day and the kids didn't have school.

"I don't know. What do you want to do?" Roz asked.

"I want to go to the youth center," Nathaniel said. "All the kids are hanging out there. Bobby and I want to play basketball."

The girls thought going to the youth center was a good idea, too, so Roz loaded them into the car for the short drive. The kids talked happily about their planned activities, unconcerned that their uncle had left less than an hour ago. Apparently, she was the only one with separation anxiety and abandonment issues.

Roz dropped the kids off and, twenty minutes later, she returned to the empty house. Two days ago, Paul and Nathaniel had moved her furniture back to her upstairs bedroom. Her doctors had cleared her to walk up and down the stairs without limitations, so there was no need for her to continue to sleep downstairs. It had been comforting knowing that Paul was sleeping on the other side of the wall those two nights, even though she'd had to restrain herself from giving in to temptation and going to him. They'd established that their relationship would never be romantic. The kiss they'd shared would be their last. It would feel lonely tonight, knowing that he wouldn't be sleeping a few steps away, but it was a feeling she'd have to get used to.

She climbed the stairs and then entered the guest room. Paul had stripped the bed and swept the floor before he left. There wasn't a speck of dust anywhere. Still, his presence lingered. It was as if he would return any minute. Foolishness.

There was a piece of paper propped against the lamp on the bedside table. Her name was scrawled across it in Paul's bold penmanship. Heart pounding, she picked it up and unfolded it. He'd written three words. I'll be back.

Chapter Seventeen

"Wait for your brother," Roz called for the umpteenth time. Why did she even bother? The girls were so excited, they weren't paying her any mind as they ran from one booth to the next, drawn by the attractions each one offered. Nathaniel and Bobby had promised to keep tabs on the girls, but even they were finding it hard to do as the girls ran about willy-nilly. Finally, Megan and Suzanne decided they wanted to get their faces painted and joined the kids in line.

"How are you holding up?" Charlotte asked.

Roz smiled at her friend. "Fine. I haven't had this much energy in the longest time. Which is good, considering that Suzanne has finally turned back into herself and has boundless energy."

"That's good, although that's not what I meant."

Roz brushed her hand over her hair, tucking it behind her ears. She was getting used to wearing the wig although her own hair was starting to grow back.

The family had gotten used to life without Paul and were establishing new routines. Roz had returned to work on a part-time basis and the kids spent three afternoons a week at the youth center. Megan was taking a tumbling class and now cartwheeled all over the house. Suzanne was studying ballet because she wanted to be a good dancer when she danced with the prince at the ball. Roz had told her more than once that there wouldn't be any princes at the ball, but Suzanne had insisted there would be. After a while, Roz decided that trying to convince Suzanne was a losing battle and stopped fighting. And who was she to say a prince wouldn't show up?

"Then, what did you mean?"

"How are you doing without Paul?"

Just hearing his name made Roz's heart ache. She reminded herself that she'd gotten over him before and could do it again. The time would come when she could think of him without her stomach feeling like she'd been dropped from the top of a ten-story building. Until then, she would paste on a smile and keep moving forward.

"I'm fine. We're all fine."

Charlotte stepped around a smashed cookie until she and Roz were face-to-face. Roz had no choice but to look into her friend's concerned eyes. "This is me you're talking to."

"I know." Roz blew out a breath and looked around. Although there were plenty of people milling about, they were involved in their own activities and weren't paying attention to her. She could talk freely without fear of being overheard. "I still can't believe he's gone. A couple of times I've actually called out his name to tell him something. Which just proves that I've got issues. He was only around for a few months. I'd lived without him for years. It shouldn't be so hard to get used to him being gone."

"The amount of time he was here really isn't important. What matters is what happened while he was here. You relied on him. So did the kids. You cared for each other. You became a family. That has nothing to do with time and everything to do with love."

"Love." Roz scoffed even though her hopeful heart jumped in her chest. "He didn't love me. He may have stopped hating me, which is nice, but I won't go so far as to say he loved me."

"There are different kinds of love. He loved the kids and they loved him right back. And you loved him, so don't bother to deny it. You might not agree with me, but I believe he loved you, too. Not just the concern type of love, but romantic love."

"Which is why he isn't here now. He promised to come back so we could take the kids around this weekend, and he didn't show up. I guess hanging around us isn't as exciting as being back in Florida and sailing his yacht." Yeah, that was snarky and sarcastic, but Roz couldn't help it. What Charlotte said sounded good, and it would be easy to get sucked into believing it. But she couldn't. She had to protect her heart.

"I thought you said he called when he got back to Florida. And that he checks in from time to time."

"He did. And he does," Roz admitted. "But most of our conversations are pretty bland. He spends a lot of time talking to the kids, too. I bet his old girlfriend convinced him to give her a second chance and he doesn't know how to tell me." Something he'd never been willing to give her. "Or maybe he doesn't think it matters since our relationship was never going to be anything more."

"I doubt it."

"I don't. I've seen pictures of them together. She's gorgeous. And smart. She's a neurosurgeon, you know. For all I know, they could be on a romantic getaway right now." Her stomach seized as she said the words. She didn't want Paul to be on a romantic vacation with another woman, even if it was all in Roz's mind.

"She couldn't be all that important to him if he stayed away from her for months on end."

"You don't know that," Roz countered, even though she hoped Charlotte was right. It wouldn't change a thing in her life, but she hated the thought of Paul being in love with anyone but her. And didn't that make her the most selfish person on the planet.

"Of course I do. I love Rick. And I trust him. But you'd better believe there is no way I would let him go off and leave me behind while he took care of his ex-girlfriend and her kids."

Roz shrugged, trying to stamp out the hope that Charlotte's words created inside her heart. "Technically, I was his former sister-in-law."

"That's not my point."

"What is your point?"

"My point is that's no way to have a relationship. I don't believe he went back to that woman."

"Then why did he leave me?" That question kept her up nights and echoed through her mind all day.

"Did you ask him to stay?"

"Of course not."

"Why not?"

Roz turned away from Charlotte's question and focused on her girls, who had made it to the front of the line and were in the midst of getting their faces painted. Megan was being transformed into a kitten, while Suzanne was being turned into a fairy. "Because it wouldn't be fair. He has a life in Florida. I can't ask him to give it all up for me."

"Is that the only reason?"

Roz frowned. This is what happened when you shared the most painful events of your past with friends. They didn't let you lie to them. Or yourself. "No. I was afraid he would turn me down. Or worse, that he would promise to come back and then let me down again. I can't open myself up to that kind of hurt again. My heart can't take the disappointment."

"But what if you don't get hurt this time? Maybe things didn't work out before because you guys were too young. But you're both older. And wiser. Look at Rick and me. He left me standing at the altar years ago because he wasn't ready to get married. Things didn't work out between us before, but we're getting married in a few weeks. What if this is the right time for you and Paul?"

"It's nothing like what happened between you and Rick. Even if he doesn't go back to his girlfriend, it doesn't change the fact that I married his half brother."

"Nothing in the past will change. Surely, Paul has learned that by now. And I hope you know that, too."

"I do." Which was why she didn't share Charlotte's optimism.

"Then let it go," Charlotte continued. "Stop letting the past be an obstacle to the future. Instead, start planning a way to get your man back."

Roz smiled, and for the first time since Paul left, she could breathe without her heart aching. Charlotte was right. Roz needed to let Paul know how she felt.

She had to summon up the courage to tell him that she loved him and ask for a second chance. And if he still didn't want her? Well, it would hurt, but she would survive. And she'd be able to go into her future without regrets.

"You look so pretty, Mommy," Suzanne said as she and Megan walked into Roz's bedroom.

Roz smiled at her youngest daughter. Dressed in a red dress she'd picked out herself and the shiniest red shoes they could find, Suzanne did indeed look like a princess. "Thanks, baby. I need to look my best if I want to be as pretty as you and Megan."

Both girls giggled and twisted at the waist, sending their skirts swirling around their calves. Although the girls had initially wanted long dresses, "to the floor" as Megan described it, Roz had convinced them that tea length was the way to go. The girls had pouted until Roz pointed out that their pretty shoes would be hidden beneath a full-length dress. Then they'd gotten on board and enthusiastically tried on dress after dress until they'd settled on these.

They were so proud of their appearances, especially their brand-new high-heeled shoes. One inch wasn't much to Roz, but to little girls it was the difference between being a little kid and being a big kid. And they definitely wanted to be counted among the big kids tonight.

"You're the prettiest of all," Megan said, brushing

a hand against the skirt of her royal blue dress. She lifted one black patent leather shoe and inspected it for dust. Apparently satisfied with the state of her shoes, she put her foot back on the floor.

"I like your hair," Suzanne said. Suzanne had remarked on Roz's new style several times a day over the past couple of weeks. Only time would tell how her daughter would react once she ditched the wig and wore a new, shorter do.

"Thank you." Roz checked herself in the mirror. The silver fabric shimmered in the light. The top was fitted across her breasts and skimmed her stomach before giving way to a full skirt, showing off her now-returned curves. The dress had been on sale, but she would have paid full price. Tonight was the beginning of her new happier and healthier life. "Is your brother ready?"

"I don't know. He's in his room." The girls came to stand beside Roz so they could admire themselves in the full-length mirror. They turned from side to side, smiling with pleasure at their reflections. Roz had found rhinestone tiaras and each girl was wearing one, their thick hair down, brushing against their shoulder blades.

"I'll go check on him," Roz said, although she was not sure either girl had heard her. She wondered if she would be able to pull them away from the mirror when it was time to leave.

Nathaniel's door was closed, so she knocked.

When he didn't answer, she turned the knob and poked her head inside. He was sitting on the edge of his bed, glaring at the tie in his hand.

"Is everything all right?" she asked, even though she could tell it wasn't.

"I don't know how to do this," he said, holding up the tie. "I thought Uncle Paul would be here and he could help me. He told me on the phone that he would be, but he's not."

Roz's heart sank as she felt her son's pain. "He wanted to be here, but you know he told us that a fire broke out in one of his fitness clubs and he had to take care of things. Do you miss him?"

One side of Nathaniel's mouth lifted in a half smile. "I do. It was cool having him around, but I knew he couldn't stay forever."

"That's right. But we can call him from time to time."

"I know." Nathaniel's eyes lit up and he smiled broadly. "Don't forget. He's going to take me fishing on his boat."

"I remember." She hoped Paul would keep that promise.

"Hey, do you think Bobby could come, too? He's never been fishing off a boat either."

"It wouldn't hurt to ask." She took the tie from his hand. He looked so mature in his navy suit. So much like a man. "Now let's take care of tying this."

"Do you know how?"

She shook her head. “No. But I bet we can find a video on YouTube. They have everything there.”

He followed her downstairs to the computer. Now that she was sleeping in her old bedroom, she’d converted the downstairs bedroom into an office. Sure enough, there was a video explaining, step by step, how to correctly make a Windsor knot in the tie. After a couple of false starts, Nathaniel mastered it and his tie looked perfect. Her heart filled with pride at the young man he was becoming.

She and Nathaniel managed to pry the girls away from the mirror and then drove to the youth center. There were several restaurants in town, but none of them was large enough to hold the entire population at the same time. The youth center not only had sufficient space, it was well equipped to handle the messes and spills that were inevitable with children.

Luck was with them and they found a parking spot near the front door. She turned off the car, released her seat belt and started to open her car door.

“Wait,” Nathaniel commanded, touching her arm. “I’ll get your door for you. I’ll open everyone’s door.”

Roz smiled. “Thanks. You are such a gentleman.”

Nathaniel’s pride was evident as he helped Roz and his sisters from the car, then carefully closed the doors behind them. He took each of his sisters by the hand and looked up at Roz, a lopsided grin on his face. “Sorry. I only have two hands.”

Megan giggled. "That's what you always say, Mommy."

"It's true, and not just for me." Roz took Megan's free hand and the four of them trekked to the door. It swung open, and a handsome teenager in a gray suit held it open for them. "Thanks."

Suzanne and Megan gasped. "Wow," they said simultaneously.

Wow indeed. Roz looked around in amazement. The youth center had been transformed into every romantic fantasy she'd ever dared to dream. Twinkling white lights dangled from plants and hung from the ceiling as if by magic threads. Yards and yards of gold and white fabric covered the walls. White roses spilling from urns perfumed the air. And they were only in the entrance.

"I'm going to find Bobby, okay?" Nathaniel asked. Obviously, he believed his duty as a gentleman ended when he'd ushered the females of his family inside the building. "Okay, Mom?" he repeated when she didn't answer quickly enough.

She nodded. "Be good."

"Do you suppose the princes are here?" Suzanne whispered, her hands pressed hopefully against her chest.

Nathaniel rolled his eyes before running off to find his friend. Clearly, he was unaffected by the surroundings. But then he'd never cared for fairy tales in the same way his sisters did.

"I hope so," Megan replied before Roz could. "I might marry one."

"Not me," Suzanne said firmly. "I'm going to marry Uncle Paul."

Just hearing Paul's name made Roz's heart skip a beat. She didn't comment, though, because she couldn't speak over the lump in her throat. When he'd left, she hadn't believed he would come back. He'd managed to convince her in their conversations. But that was before the fire. Her rational mind knew that he wasn't going to show. So why was she still hoping that he would magically materialize?

Because she was a fool, that's why. Well, enough foolishness. She had children to raise. Daughters to teach that they didn't need a prince to rescue them. She needed to show them that they could have a happy and fulfilled life without being coupled with someone else. The best way to do that was by example.

She took each one by the hand. "Come on, girls. Let's go find the ballroom. I want to see just how beautiful that is. And then we can find the kids' party."

Smiling at two men dressed in tuxedos, Roz led the girls through the hallways and to the gym. Again, the decorations took her breath away. She'd been to fancy hotels before and had seen many beautiful rooms, but the gym in all of its glory put them to shame. She could have been standing inside the fairy castle of one of the girls' favorite stories. She foolishly began to wonder if maybe happily-ever-after did happen in real life and could happen for her. Of course, since she was short one fairy godmother, that could be a problem. But it was a problem for another day. Tonight was for fun and maybe a little bit of dreaming.

"Well, don't you all look beautiful?" Charlotte said. Somehow her best friend had materialized while Roz was looking around.

"Thanks." Roz rubbed her hands over her silver dress. For the first time in months she felt like a whole woman. A sexy woman. "You look great yourself."

"This old thing?" Charlotte asked, then laughed. Charlotte had a strict exercise regimen although her diet was that of an eleven-year-old. She looked fabulous in a long white dress that clung to her body like a second skin. If she didn't know how good she looked, Roz would have felt like a scarecrow standing next to Charlotte. "Let's just agree that we're the belles of the ball, shall we?"

"Absolutely," Roz agreed, although the other women in attendance did look spectacular. The dresses were in every color of the rainbow, but black seemed to be a favorite choice. Many women were draped in stunning jewels. Roz wore simple diamond studs and a diamond tennis bracelet that had belonged to her mother that her great-aunt, in a rare show of kindness, had saved for Roz.

"The kids are set up down the hall in the cafeteria. The teenagers are in charge, although parents are rotating in and out to make sure the kids behave themselves. Rick is scheduled for now. Shall we drop off the girls and then mingle? From the amount of attention you're drawing from the single men, I think you're going to be busy in a few minutes."

Roz didn't answer. She'd noticed a few heads turn in her direction when she'd entered the room. She didn't expect to feel anything special for any of the men, but she was open to the possibility that one might make her feel a slight zing. Maybe her heart wouldn't sing as it had when she was with Paul, but it might hum a few notes. She would never know if she didn't try.

She smiled and nodded at a few people she recognized as she led the girls to the kids' party. Once again, the decorations, although different from the ones in the ballroom, were spectacular. There was an enormous arch constructed of silver and gold balloons in one corner of the room, and several preteen girls were clustered there. The seats of folding chairs had been covered with gold and silver fabric, and an alternating silver or gold balloon had been tied to the backs of the chairs. A photographer had been hired and she was walking around taking candid pictures.

Megan and Suzanne squealed when they saw their

friends and joined them at the punch bowl in the center of a festively decorated table. Clearly, a mother had been in charge of the liquid refreshment, and instead of the expected red, which created indelible stains on all kinds of clothes, the punch was frothy and clear. There were plates filled with cake, brownies, chocolate chip cookies and other assorted goodies, so, the punch notwithstanding, there was undoubtedly a visit to the dry cleaner in her future.

As with most dances for the junior high set, the boys were huddled together on one wall, laughing and talking, completely oblivious to the girls, who were giggling and sneaking glances at them. If Nathaniel's declaration about only dancing with his sisters was any indication of how the other boys felt, the girls were either going to have to do the asking or dance with each other. The six- and seven-year-old girls didn't seem to have a problem doing that, as Megan, Suzanne and their friends were already on the dance floor, bumping into each other as they tried to perform the complicated movements of a line dance.

Roz waved to the kids, then walked back to the ballroom with Charlotte. "Do you think the boys will get out there and dance?"

Charlotte laughed. "Not a chance. Bobby insisted that I was the only girl he was going to dance with. Apparently, a girl passed him a note in school asking him to be her boyfriend. She even tried to hold his hand. Rick thinks it's no big deal. I think that little girl needs to sit down somewhere and leave my Bobby alone."

"I'm with Rick," Roz said, biting her lip in order to keep from laughing at the outraged expression on her friend's face. "It's cute. You're just worried that you'll lose your status as Bobby's best girl."

Charlotte shook her head. "That's ridiculous."

"It sure is. That boy loves you. His love won't fade when he starts liking girls and wants to hold their hands. You know that's not how love works." And didn't she know that better than anyone? Her love for Paul was as strong as it had been a decade ago. Although she'd chosen not to act on that love and had hidden it in a tiny part of her heart, she knew that if given the opportunity to flourish, it would bloom like a rose in summer.

But if she was going to find love in the future, she needed to find a way to bury it once and for all. She needed to open her heart to the possibility of falling in love with a new man.

"Come on," she said, tugging on Charlotte's arm. "I feel like dancing the night away. Or until ten thirty, when the dance ends."

Paul walked into the youth center, momentarily stunned by the transformation. They'd taken decorating to another level. No doubt many women stepped inside and immediately started fantasizing about meeting their Prince Charming tonight. Paul wouldn't be surprised if a marriage proposal or two resulted from the events of the night. And he predicted that more than one baby would be born nine months from now.

Not that any of that mattered to him. All he cared about was getting to Roz. It had been far too long since he'd seen her. He'd been to the youth center many times with the kids, so he knew his way around. He followed the sound of music and laughter down the hall. From the look of things, the party was in full swing. Thank goodness he wasn't too late.

He stepped around a pillar that had been wrapped in white lights and didn't seem to serve a purpose other than impeding his progress. Blowing out a breath, he tamped down his irritation and tried to stop frowning. He didn't want Roz to think he was angry with her.

Nothing had gone according to plan. He'd intended to be back in town two days ago so he and Roz could take the kids to the carnival and parade. But there'd been a fire in one of his gyms in Virginia, started when the barbecue joint next door went up in flames. The fire had occurred after hours and the building had been empty, so, thankfully, no one had been injured. The damage had been substantial and the club would be closed for several weeks while repairs were done.

Roz had been disappointed when he'd told her he

wouldn't be able to make it. Though she'd claimed to understand, he knew she was thinking the past was repeating itself. Which was why he hadn't told her he was coming to the ball tonight. Just in case something went wrong, which it had, he wanted to spare her feelings.

He'd hit the road as soon as he could, but that was later than he would have liked. He'd been making good time and expected to arrive in enough time to change clothes and leave with Roz and the kids. Then he'd had a flat tire—a flat tire!—on the highway, throwing his plan to surprise Roz at the house out the window. Fortunately, he'd been wearing jeans and hadn't gotten his tuxedo dirty. He'd let himself into Roz's house, taken the quickest shower on record, changed clothes and hid his present for her in the kitchen before racing to the youth center. The parking lot was packed and he'd had to park so far from the entrance that he could have left the car at Roz's house and walked.

He passed a few women he vaguely recognized and nodded, not slowing his pace. His heart began to thump in his chest as he realized he would soon be seeing Roz. He'd missed her. Being away from her had clarified his thinking and proved one thing: she was in his blood. He'd realized that he would die if he didn't have Roz in his life.

He didn't know why things hadn't worked out before, but that no longer mattered. Blaming Roz for every mistake she'd made didn't work for him any longer. He wanted her and needed her just as much as he needed the blood pumping in his veins. Maybe more.

Stepping into the converted ballroom, he scanned the crowd. A jazz ensemble was playing a slow, romantic song and many couples swayed to the music. The room was dimly lit, so it was difficult to see clearly. And then he saw her. She was in the arms of another man, smiling into his face. An ache hit his heart so hard, it felt as if a five-hundred-pound weight had been dropped on his chest. Could he be too late?

They turned, and Paul got a glimpse of the other man's face. Russell Danielson, Joni's brother and Nathaniel's chosen husband for his mother. The kid had told Paul he'd planned to get them together. Paul hadn't believed Nathaniel would be able to pull it off. He'd been wrong. More important, he hadn't thought Roz would be interested in seeing another man so soon.

Why had he thought that? Did he really believe Roz was going to wait around for him to figure out what he wanted? Especially since he hadn't been clear that he wanted her. In fact, he'd done the opposite. He'd told her that he wasn't interested in revisiting the past. That he would never allow himself to love her again. Was it so unexpected that she would look to someone else for love? Not that he thought she and Russell were in love. Still, he didn't like seeing another man with his arms around her.

He didn't fight for her last time. When he'd learned that Roz was planning to marry Terrence, he should have come home. He should have done whatever it took to convince her that he loved her and that they belonged together. Instead, he'd let his pride get in the way and he'd done nothing. Over the years, he'd grown angrier and more bitter.

Not this time. He might not be the world's smartest man, but he wasn't a fool either. There was no way he was going to stand aside and watch her walk away with another man. He was going to do whatever it took to win Roz's heart.

He took a step, determination driving him. A small hand gripped his and he stopped. Looking down, he saw Suzanne's smiling face. Megan stood next to her, her eyes wide with surprise. She let out a little squeal then jumped up and down, clapping her hands. "You're here, Uncle Paul."

"I told you he was coming," Suzanne said, nudging her sister. "You just didn't believe me." Suzanne turned shining eyes to him. "I believed you were coming, and here you are. You look just like a prince. Are you going to dance with me now?"

"And me?" Megan asked.

"Absolutely," Paul replied, noticing for the first time that the room was filling up with children and teenagers. He spotted Nathaniel with Bobby, but his nephew's eyes were glued to his mother and he didn't see Paul. Grinning, Nathaniel poked Bobby in the side and then pointed at Roz and Russell. Apparently, he thought his plan was working. Paul hated to disappoint the kid, but he was going to be the one who won Roz's love.

"We're coming in here so we can dance with our moms and dads," Megan said.

"And special people. Mom asked Dr. Rick to be our special person, but I want you to be my special person," Suzanne said.

"Mine, too," Megan added. "We like Dr. Rick because he's nice, but we love you."

Paul's throat suddenly felt clogged with emotion and he could barely speak above a whisper. He cleared his throat. "I love you girls, too. And I would be honored to be your special person."

"And Mommy's," Suzanne added. "Don't you want to be Mommy's special person, too?"

Paul looked back at the dance floor. "Yes. I definitely want to be your mom's special person."

The song ended and the overhead lights switched on. Mayor Devlin stood on a makeshift stage and spoke into a microphone.

"Thank you all for coming to our inaugural Sweet Briar ball, capping off our first ever Sweet Briar harvest festival. The feedback I've received from visitors and business owners alike has been remarkable. In short, the festival was an unqualified success. We could not have done it without your support. I'm not going to make a long speech, but I do want to recognize Charlotte Shields and thank her for all of her hard work."

There was prolonged applause and cheers. Charlotte joined the mayor on the stage and accepted a bouquet of flowers before waving and stepping back so the mayor could continue with his remarks.

"Now it's time for the mother and son and father and daughter dances."

"And special people," Megan called out.

"And special people," the mayor added. "And for those of you with more than one child, don't worry. There will be seven special dances. If that's not enough for people to dance with their kids, I'm going to suggest some of you get hobbies."

There was laughter and then parents and kids began to seek each other out. Nathaniel raced to Roz and led her off the dance floor. The girls ran to greet them and Paul followed.

She was so beautiful. He'd never get enough of looking at her. She was smiling at something Nathaniel said, her face glowing with joy. Then she looked at Paul and stumbled, freezing for the tiniest moment. Her smile faded and her nose wrinkled in confusion. Clearly, she hadn't expected him to return. That reaction hurt, but he knew he'd earned it. He also knew it would take time and effort to gain her trust. Whatever it took, whatever she needed, he was willing to do.

Nathaniel looked from Roz to Paul. "Hey, Uncle Paul. I didn't know you were here."

"I'm a little late." Paul turned from his nephew to look at Roz. "You look absolutely beautiful."

She smiled and the nerves that had been churning his stomach diminished. "Thank you."

He wanted to say more, but before he could, the music began to play. Nathaniel took Roz's hand. "Are you ready to dance with me?"

"Of course."

"No. Wait. That was wrong." He bowed a little at the waist. "May I have this dance, Mom?"

Roz's pleased smile warmed Paul's heart. He watched proudly as Nathaniel led his mother to the floor.

"I understand that I'm supposed to be a special person," Rick said, joining Paul and the girls. "But since your uncle is here, I don't know if my services are needed."

"We're dancing with Uncle Paul," Suzanne confirmed, grabbing Paul by the hand. Megan quickly grabbed the other one.

"How about we take turns? You can dance with me and Dr. Rick," Paul suggested.

"Okay," the girls answered in unison.

Paul danced with Suzanne while Megan danced with Rick. When the song ended, they switched partners. Each girl was ecstatic to dance in the big room with him and chattered happily, filling him in on their night. They'd eaten desserts and drunk frothy punch. As promised, Nathaniel had danced with each of them twice. He'd even convinced Bobby to dance with them once. But they each claimed it was so much better to dance with him. He enjoyed it, too, but he had a feeling he was being set up. Not that he minded.

When the second dance ended, Nathaniel escorted his mother back to Paul. The girls giggled and stared. Megan asked, "Aren't you going to dance with Mommy? She's special."

"Of course I'm going to dance with your mom."

"Girls, this dance is for parents and kids so—" Roz started, but he cut her off. He wasn't going to let her wiggle out of this dance when he was dying to hold her in his arms and feel her body pressed up against his.

"—and special people," Paul added, his eyes searching her face.

"You don't have to," Roz said. He saw the wariness in her eyes. The doubt. He'd done that to her. And he'd have to fix it. Starting with this dance.

He mimicked Nathaniel, bowing at the waist. Rising, he extended his hand. "May I have this dance?"

"Say yes," Suzanne urged.

Roz looked at her children, who were grinning broadly. Megan even gave her a little push. Several people who were standing nearby watched, as well. Good. He may as well let all the other men in Sweet Briar know Roz was unavailable. She nodded and he released a relieved breath. "Yes. I'd love to."

Taking her by her hand, he led her to the dance floor, then took her into his arms. She held herself stiff for a moment and then breathed out a sigh before relaxing against him. Her breasts were soft against his chest and his heart skipped a beat. It felt so good to hold her in his arms. So right. He truly believed she was made for him. Or rather, they were made for each other. They fit together like puzzle pieces. Two halves of a whole. The thought didn't seem as ridiculous as he'd once believed.

He pulled her more snugly against his chest and her delicate scent wafted around him. As usual, she wasn't wearing perfume, but she didn't need it. Her own heady scent had him wishing they were alone and he could show her just how much she meant to him.

He closed his eyes and let the music carry him away. The song ended and people around them moved and switched partners, perhaps to dance with a different special person. Roz started to step away, but Paul tightened his hold on her. She leaned back and looked at him, puzzlement in her beautiful brown eyes. "One more dance?"

She nodded, then lay her head on his shoulder.

Oh, yeah. They were meant to be together. They had a few details to iron out, but the future was looking bright. Very bright indeed.

Chapter Eighteen

Roz sighed. She could stay in Paul's arms forever. She felt so right there. So loved. Of course, those feelings were only an illusion, but wasn't every woman allotted at least one fantasy in her lifetime? On a perfect night like this, she would pretend that it wasn't only a dream and that Paul shared her feelings. For this fleeting moment in time, she wouldn't worry about what the future held or try to figure out where—if anywhere—they would go from here.

She didn't squelch the hope that being this close to Paul stirred in her. Paul had come back to Sweet Briar for the ball. Surely, that had to mean something. If he didn't care about her, would he have come back? She wanted to say yes, but she knew that wasn't necessarily true. He'd promised the girls he'd come back and he'd kept that promise. He'd also committed to dancing with her, hence the dance they were now sharing. But he'd only promised one dance. They were on their third.

She inhaled deeply, and his scent floated around her before settling in her heart like rose petals landing on the soft earth. Her heart was full and she realized just how deeply she loved him. It made no sense to pretend that she could put this love behind her and find a way to love someone else.

There had to be hope for them. If he couldn't see it yet, then she'd show him. One thing was certain—she wasn't going to let him walk away from her without a fight. She'd fought cancer and won. She'd fight for Paul's heart and she'd win that battle, too.

The music ended and she reluctantly pulled out of Paul's arms and away from the warmth of his body. She glanced into his eyes, surprised by the longing she saw there. It mirrored hers. "Thanks."

"The pleasure was all mine," Paul said.

"No, it wasn't. I enjoyed those dances. And I wouldn't mind a few more."

"We'll definitely have to make that happen."

"The sooner, the better," she said with a smile.

Wrapping his arm around her waist, he led her to the kids, who were watching every move they made, broad grins on their faces.

"Looks like the ball is about over," Paul said. "You guys ready to go home?"

"Can we say bye to our friends first?" Megan asked.

"And I want to get some cookies for the road," Nathaniel added.

"Okay," Roz replied. "Just make it quick."

The kids scurried away, leaving Roz alone with Paul. Her skin tingled where his hand rested on the small of her back. Nothing in the world could make her step away from him.

"Thanks for coming," she said. "I know that, with everything going on, this wasn't the most convenient time for you to be here."

"I've got people who can handle the business in my absence."

"But—"

"No buts. I'm exactly where I want to be and doing exactly what I want to do."

Before she could ask him what he meant, Nathaniel skidded to a stop in front of Paul, his sisters right behind him. "We're ready to go."

"I'm parked near the door," Roz said as they walked through the center.

"Lucky you. I'm at the far end of the lot."

They all walked to Roz's car. Paul opened the door and held it for her.

"I want to go with Uncle Paul," Megan said.

"Me, too," Suzanne piped up, grabbing his free hand.

"Okay," Paul said before she could reply. "I'd like the company."

"I'll ride with you, Mom," Nathaniel said, climbing into the passenger seat.

"See you at home," Paul said, closing her door.

Home. She liked the sound of it. She didn't want to read too much into one simple word, but hope went coursing through her veins.

"I'm glad Uncle Paul is back," Nathaniel said. "I missed him."

"So did I," Roz confessed.

"It feels good when he's around. I like the way he helps me protect you and Megan and Suzanne."

Mixed emotions crashed through Roz. She was proud that her son wanted to take care of her and his sisters. At the same time, she was also sad that he felt compelled to take on the responsibility at his age. Thank goodness he was willing to accept another man's help. He could have resented Paul's presence, but he didn't. Nathaniel loved Paul and liked being around him. Paul had become more than her son's role model. He'd become Nathaniel's hero. Truthfully, Paul had become her hero, too.

She pulled into the driveway and waited as, once more, Nathaniel opened her car door. They'd been in the house about five minutes when Paul parked his car behind hers. Despite the amount of sugar they'd consumed, the girls had fallen asleep on the ride home, so she carried Suzanne to her room while he carried Megan. Nathaniel followed, said good-night and went to his room.

Paul placed Megan on her bed and removed her shoes, then went to the dresser and pulled out two pairs of pajamas. "Need help?" he asked Roz.

"Nope. I've got it."

"I'll meet you downstairs in a minute, then."

"It'll take me a couple of minutes to change."

One corner of his mouth lifted. "I was kind of hoping you would keep on that dress a little while longer. I really like it."

Warmth flowed through her veins like honey. "Only if you leave on that tuxedo."

"Deal."

Ten minutes later, she joined Paul in the living room. Soft music played from a Bluetooth speaker. He'd dimmed the lights and candles flickered from where he placed them around the room. A vase of red roses was in the center of the coffee table. A wrapped box was beside it.

"What's in the box?"

He laughed. "It's a present."

"For me?"

"Yes. I brought gifts for the kids, too, but since they're asleep they won't get to open theirs until tomorrow." He handed her the package. "Since you're awake, you can have yours now."

The box was heavier than she thought it would be. Her mind raced as she began to peel away the tape to remove the paper. Although the suspense was killing her, anticipation was part of the pleasure. When the last of the tape was removed, she took off the paper. "A cuckoo clock."

"Yes." He was grinning from ear to ear.

"It's just like the one I saw when we went on the boat ride."

"It is the one we saw. I noticed how much you liked it, so I went back and got it for you."

She couldn't think of the words to express her emotions. "Thank you. I love it so much."

"You're welcome. You deserve to have something you wanted so much."

She smiled broadly. What could she say to something like that?

He offered her a mug of hot chocolate. He'd gone so far as to add whipped cream and bits of chocolate. Lifting the mug to her mouth, she took a sip and moaned.

"I take it that you like it."

"Yep." She took a seat on the sofa. First the gift and now her favorite beverage. If she didn't know better, she would think Paul was trying to seduce her. They sipped their drinks in silence, enjoying each other's company.

When they finished, he took her cup, placed it on the table and then held her hand. He stroked his fingers over her palm and tingles raced up her spine. "I missed you."

"Really?"

"Why do you sound so surprised?"

"I'm not just surprised. I'm confused about what's going on between us. We kissed like it meant something, but a minute later you were adamant that we weren't in love and didn't have a future together." She considered mentioning Kristin but decided she didn't need a third person in the room. The other woman didn't really have anything to do with Roz and Paul's relationship.

"I wasn't sure what I felt. The girls were talking about us getting married and that kind of talk made me a little nervous then."

"I understand. You have a business to focus on."

"Then, Roz. I wasn't sure then. I know exactly what I want now."

"And what is that?"

He smiled at her. "Don't you know?"

She shook her head, her heart thumping against her rib cage. She needed to hear him say it.

"You. I want you. I love you, Roz. I fell in love with you when I was a boy. We were too young to make a lasting commitment. Too young to follow through. For years I tried to get over you. I'd even convinced myself that I hated you. But that was a lie. I've never stopped loving you. And I don't think I ever will. I don't want to."

Tears filled her eyes. She let them fall.

"Please tell me those are happy tears," Paul whispered.

"The happiest of all." Her voice wobbled. "I love you, too."

He blew out a breath and she realized that he must have been worried about her response. "Good."

"So how are we going to make this work? You live and work in Florida. The kids have been through so much I can't see myself uprooting them."

"You don't have to. Well, we might think about getting a bigger house at some time in the future. One with more bathrooms. But I'm going to be moving here."

"You are?"

"Yes. I like Sweet Briar. Besides, the woman I love lives here."

Roz grinned. The past few months had been rough, but they'd made it through together. She knew that, whatever the future held, they would get by the same way. Paul might not be a prince, but it looked like she was getting her happily-ever-after.

* * * * *

Don't miss a single story
in Kathy Douglass's
Sweet Briar Sweethearts series:

COMING NEXT MONTH FROM

HARLEQUIN

SPECIAL EDITION

Available August 18, 2020

#2785 THE MAVERICK'S BABY ARRANGEMENT

Montana Mavericks: What Happened to Beatrix?
by Kathy Douglass

In order to retain custody of his eight-month-old niece, Daniel Dubois convinces event planner and confirmed businesswoman Brittany Brandt to marry him. It's only supposed to be a mutually beneficial business agreement...*if* they can both keep their hearts out of the equation.

#2786 THE LAST MAN SHE EXPECTED

Welcome to Starlight • by Michelle Major

When Mara Reed agrees to partner with her sworn enemy, Parker Johnson, to help a close friend, she doesn't expect the feelings of love and tenderness that complicate every interaction with the handsome attorney. Will Mara and Parker risk everything for love?

#2787 CHANGING HIS PLANS

Gallant Lake Stories • by Jo McNally

Real estate developer Brittany Doyle is eager to bring the mountain town of Gallant Lake into the twenty-first century...by changing everything. Hardware store owner Nate Thomas hates change. These opposites refuse to compromise, except when it comes to falling in love.

#2788 A WINNING SEASON

Wickham Falls Weddings • by Rochelle Alers

When Sutton Reed returns to Wickham Falls after finishing a successful baseball career, he assumes he'll just join the family business and live an uneventful life. Until his neighbor's younger brother tries to steal his car, that is. Now he's finding himself mentoring the boy—and being drawn to Zoey Allen like no one else.

#2789 IN SERVICE OF LOVE

Sutter Creek, Montana • by Laurel Greer

Commitmentphobic veterinarian Maggie is focused on training a Great Dane as a service dog and expanding the family dog-training business. Can widowed single dad Asher's belief in love after loss inspire Maggie to risk her heart and find forever with the irresistible librarian?

#2790 THE SLOW BURN

Masterson, Texas • by Caro Carson

When firefighter Caden Sterling unexpectedly delivers Tana McKenna's baby by the side of the road, the unlikely threesome forms a special bond. Their flirty friendship slowly becomes more, until Tana's ex and the truth about her baby catches up with her. Can she win back the only man who can make this family complete?

SPECIAL EXCERPT FROM

HARLEQUIN

SPECIAL EDITION

Real estate developer Brittany Doyle is eager to bring the mountain town of Gallant Lake into the twenty-first century...by changing everything. Hardware store owner Nate Thomas hates change. These opposites refuse to compromise, except when it comes to falling in love.

Read on for a sneak peek at
Changing His Plans,
the next book in the Gallant Lake Stories miniseries by Jo McNally.

He stuck his head around the corner of the fasteners aisle just in time to see a tall brunette stagger into the revolving seed display. Some of the packets went flying, but she managed to steady the display before the whole thing toppled. He took in what probably had been a very nice silk blouse and tailored trouser suit before she was drenched in the storm raging outside. The heel on one of the ridiculously high heels she was wearing had snapped off, explaining why she was stumbling around.

"Having a bad morning?"

The woman looked up in annoyance, strands of dark, wet hair falling across her face.

"You could say that. I don't suppose you have a shoe repair place in this town?" She looked at the bright red heel in her hand.

Nate shook his head as he approached her. "Nope. But hand it over. I'll see what I can do."

A perfectly shaped brow arched high. "Why? Are you going to cobble them back together with—" she gestured around widely "—maybe some staples or screws?"

"Technically, what you just described is the definition of cobbling, so yeah. I've got some glue that'll do the trick." He met her gaze calmly. "It'd be a lot easier to do if you'd take the shoe off. Unless you also think I'm a blacksmith?"

He was teasing her. Something about this soaking-wet woman still having so much…regal bearing…amused Nate. He wasn't usually a fan of the pearl-clutching country club set who strutted through Gallant Lake on the weekends and referred to his family's hardware store as "adorable." But he couldn't help admiring this woman's ability to hold on to her superiority while looking like she accidentally went to a water park instead of the business meeting she was dressed for. To be honest, he also admired the figure that expensive red suit was clinging to as it dripped water on his floor.

He held out his hand. "I'm Nate Thomas. This is my store."

She let out an irritated sigh. "Brittany Doyle." She slid her long, slender hand into his and gripped with surprising strength. He held it for just a half second longer than necessary before shaking off the odd current of interest she invoked in him.